To my son Leif: ninja warrior,
walking Google, and my guide
to elementary school

CAROLYN MACKLER

NOT IF I CAN HELP IT

SCHOLASTIC

Published in the UK by Scholastic, 2021
Euston House, 24 Eversholt Street, London, NW1 1DB
Scholastic Ireland, 89E Lagan Road, Dublin Industrial Estate, Glasnevin,
Dublin, D11 HP5F

SCHOLASTIC and associated logos are trademarks and/or
registered trademarks of Scholastic Inc.

First published in the US by Scholastic Press, an imprint of Scholastic Inc., 2019

Text © Carolyn Mackler, 2019
Book design by Nina Goffi

The right of Carolyn Mackler to be identified
as the author of this work has been asserted by her under the Copyright, Designs
and Patents Act 1988.

ISBN 978 0702 31091 1

A CIP catalogue record for this book is available from the British Library.

Printed by CPI Group (UK) Ltd, Croydon, CR0 4YY
Paper made from wood grown in sustainable forests and other controlled
sources.

1 3 5 7 9 10 8 6 4 2

www.scholastic.co.uk

CHAPTER 1

"Want to do best part worst part?" Ruby asks as we turn right on Broadway. She's just texted her mom that we've left school and will be at I Scream in ten minutes.

"Sure," I say, smiling as two terriers trot past us, their rhinestone collars sparkling in the sunlight. I once told Ruby how my mom and I do best part worst part every night on the phone and now she likes doing it too. "I can go first," I add. "My best part is definitely now."

Ruby's phone chimes in her pocket and she takes it out for a quick glance. I look into her hand. It's her mom saying *Okay!* with a bunch of hearts after it. Ruby is still ten and already has a phone and I'm eleven and don't have one yet. My dad says I'll get one at the beginning of sixth grade in the fall.

"Be more specific about what you mean by *now*, Willa," Ruby says, pinching her nose so she sounds congested. She's imitating our fifth-grade teacher, Ms. Lacey, who has seasonal allergies. Ms. Lacey spent the morning sneezing and coughing and lecturing us about how we can't get away with generalizations like *I dunno* and *fine*.

Ruby knows that Ms. Lacey's long lectures make me antsy, just like I know that she has to pee twice as often as the average person. Ruby Kapoor and I know so much about each other because we're best friends. We met last fall, when she and her mom moved to Manhattan from Connecticut. Now it's the spring of fifth grade, which I really don't want to think about because any day now we're going to get our middle school acceptance letters in the mail and find out where we're going to sixth grade. For one, I hate any kind of change, so the idea of leaving The Children's School, where I've gone since kindergarten, freaks me out. For two, what if Ruby and I get into different middle schools and have to be ripped apart after only one year of best friendship? That would be the worst kind of change ever.

I reach down and adjust my left sock so it's not bunched up in my sneaker. "Specifically . . . my best part is right now," I say. "Walking to I Scream with you to get ice cream—"

"And sorbet," Ruby interjects. She's lactose intolerant and has to be careful not to eat dairy or she'll get a stomachache.

"And sorbet," I add, "and definitely with a heap of gummy bears on top. Is that specific enough?"

"Yum!" Ruby says, grinning.

That was how our friendship began, with gummy bears from the exact I Scream we are walking to right now. Last August, my dad told me that a new girl was starting at The

2

Children's School and that the principal had asked a bunch of parents to take their kids to I Scream on a Sunday afternoon to meet her and greet her and make sure she felt comfortable on the first day. The new girl turned out to be Ruby—short and skinny, her long hair in a ponytail, a palate expander on her teeth. A few other girls were there, like the twins, Norie and Zoe Robbins, and horrible Avery Tanaka, smiling wide like she was going to be noticed by a talent scout while choosing her flavors. Ruby was with her mom, who was shaking hands and collecting parents' phone numbers. As we were at the toppings bar, I noticed that Ruby and I both loaded our dishes with gummy bears. I squealed and told her that gummy bears were MY signature topping. No one else understood how perfectly they stiffened when they made contact with ice cream. *Or sorbet*, she said, grinning at me. I grinned back at her, and it was best friends at first sight.

"What was *your* best part today?" I now ask Ruby as we pause at the light on Ninety-Fourth and Broadway. We live in a neighborhood of Manhattan called the Upper West Side. The exciting thing about this spring is that, after eleven years of being taken everywhere by a parent or babysitter, my dad has finally agreed to let me walk the dozen blocks to and from school by myself. I usually still walk to school with my dad and my little brother, Benji, who is eight. Going home, I sometimes walk with Benji and our sitter, Joshua, or Ruby if we have plans to hang out after school. Ruby and her mom live thirty blocks downtown, so she's not allowed to travel home by herself yet because that would mean taking the subway or a city bus, and her mom says "no way" to that. If Ruby doesn't come to my apartment, she goes to afterschool until her mom picks her up after work.

Today Joshua is taking Benji to his climbing class, and Ruby and I are meeting my dad and her mom at I Scream. My dad told me the plan this morning at breakfast, and he said that Ruby's mom was telling Ruby the same plan. They're both getting off work early, and we're supposed to leave school together and walk up there.

"My best part is also now," Ruby says. "And playing soccer at gym. That was awesome. I can't believe I got four goals! What was your worst part?"

I don't tell Ruby that soccer at gym was my worst part. I hate gym. At least at recess, I can read a book or join in a gaga game, which in my opinion is the only ball sport for people who stink at ball sports, because all you do is try to whack other people's shins with the ball while dodging the ball so your shins don't get whacked. But at gym, when participating in the sport is required, I'm forced to deal with soccer balls and volleyballs and kickballs. I can barely run without tripping, so having a ball involved in a non-gaga way makes everything worse. Unlike me, Ruby loves soccer. She plays on a team during afterschool and another team on weekends. She even watches soccer on TV, which sounds as exciting to me as watching pencils getting sharpened.

I don't want to insult soccer, so instead I ask Ruby, "Why do you think my dad and your mom want to meet us at I Scream? Don't you think that's strange on a random school day?"

Ruby shakes her head. "Probably because ice cream and sorbet covered in gummy bears is an awesome way to spend a Thursday afternoon."

I shrug. That's another way we're different. Ruby doesn't wonder why my dad and her mom would leave work early to meet us. Ruby also doesn't get upset whenever I mention middle school. She says it'll all work out. She says if we go to different middle schools, we'll stay best friends and have lots of sleepovers. The thing is, I've slept over at her apartment a bunch of times, but whenever I invite her to my apartment she makes an excuse for why she can't come. It doesn't help that I go to my mom's—she lives upstate with my stepfather—every Saturday morning and return Sunday night, so my sleepover days are limited. Even so, I can't help feeling offended that she never sleeps at my apartment. Yes, I live with two guys—my dad and brother—but they're not slobs. Actually, I'm messier than they are! My room is littered with LEGO bricks and LEGO accessories and whatever clothes I shed onto the floor in my daily quest to find something comfortable to wear.

"Maybe they want to talk to us about middle school," I say, fiddling with the bracelets on my wrist. I like to wear an assortment of stretchy bracelets, friendship bracelets, and rubber bands. "Maybe our middle school letters came

5

and they want to tell us the news together so we can celebrate if we got in to the same school and cry if we didn't."

"I doubt it," Ruby tells me. "My mom has me check the mail. All we've gotten the past few days are bills and junk mail. Nothing from the Department of Education, if that's what you're wondering."

Just then, a golden retriever walks toward us. Golden retrievers are my favorite dogs. I watch it lumber by, its feathery tail waving like a flag. Ruby is used to my dog ogling, so she gives me a second before taking my elbow and tugging me along.

"So what do you think it is?" I ask once we're walking again.

"Maybe they're planning a surprise trip to Polar Bear Adventures," Ruby offers, giggling.

"Get us some *me time*!" I say, flashing her a thumbs-up.

Ruby and I joke about the commercial for Polar Bear Adventures, an indoor water park in New Jersey. It's a cheesy commercial with the girl whooping as she whizzes down a water slide and the boy bodysurfing in a wave pool and the mom getting some "me time" in a burbling hot tub. The truth is, it actually looks fun. A few weeks ago, when my dad and brother and I had dinner with Ruby and her mom at Thai Market, we started talking about Polar Bear Adventures. Ruby's mom said maybe she'd take Ruby and me for Ruby's eleventh birthday in August. When I turned eleven in February, I had my regular birthday party—movie, pizza, and mini-cupcakes with a group of girls from school. I've been doing that since I was six. The only difference about my birthday this year was that I didn't get my big present on the actual day. That's because after years of begging, I'm finally getting a dog! My dad says we have to wait until the end of the school year to adopt one so I'll have the whole summer to bond with it.

"I guess why we're meeting them at I Scream is going to remain a mystery," Ruby concludes.

I kick at a bottle cap on the sidewalk and watch it slide into the street. "For three more blocks."

"So what was your worst part?" Ruby asks. "You still didn't say."

I'm trying to think of a worst part other than soccer at gym when we spot Avery Tanaka on the other side of Broadway. I've known Avery since preschool. She even annoyed me back when we were four and she insisted on being the queen in every castle game and the head dog in every kennel. Ruby and I glance at each other, and I can tell we're thinking the same thing: *worst part*. Across the street, Avery is eating an apple and walking toward the subway with her mom. No doubt she's going to voice lessons or tap lessons or drama coaching or whatever else Avery does to make sure she gets into a performing arts middle school and becomes a movie star someday. Aside from being horrible, Avery is perfect. She's got long, shimmery hair that's never messy, and she wears sparkly dresses and headbands and slip-on shoes, and she always gets the solo in any class performance because I think the teachers are afraid of what would happen if she didn't. It's not like I'm jealous of Avery. What bothers me is the way she rubs in her perfect life. She brags about how she has a sister in high school and they go for manicure-pedicures together, and she has a Cavalier King Charles spaniel who sleeps in her bed every night. On top of her bragging, she makes comments to me about how I still can't do a cartwheel or that I wrote my research paper on LEGOs and that's a boy topic. Even though the majority of people who trade LEGOs in my class are boys, it's not a *boy topic*. LEGOs are awesome and they're a girls' toy too. I didn't tell Avery that, though, because if I did she'd just roll her eyes and call me weird.

Avery isn't as nasty to Ruby as she is to me, except for once, when we were doing a classroom project on family trees, and she told us how sad it is that we're both from *broken homes*. My parents divorced when I was seven and Ruby's split up when she was a baby. On the way out of school that day, Ruby and I decided that Avery was wrong. Our homes aren't broken. They're just built in a different way.

Sure enough, when Avery spots Ruby and me across the street, she rises onto her tiptoes and says something into her mom's ear. A second later, Avery's mom glances in our direction and gives us an awkward wave.

"Worst part," Ruby mutters. "I have to pee, by the way."

"Didn't it look like Avery was telling her mom a secret about us?" I ask, tugging at my left sock again. It was fine all day but now it's driving me crazy. "The way she whispered and then her mom looked over?"

"She's just Avery being Avery. Can we hurry? I really have to pee."

I peer over at Avery one more time. She's tossing her apple core in the trash. As soon as she catches me watching her, she presses her lips together and grins like she knows something I don't know.

"Yeah, let's go," I tell Ruby, groaning. "Let's get out of here."

"It's just Avery being Avery," Ruby says again.

As we speed walk toward I Scream, I think about how I'm not so sure Ruby's right. It definitely looked like Avery knows something we don't know, and I don't have a good feeling about it.

CHAPTER 2

Ruby links arms with me for the rest of the way to I Scream. I try not to think about Avery smirking at us. I try not to think about all the things Avery has said to me. The year my parents got divorced, Avery was my line partner. That meant we had to hold hands everywhere our class went for the entire year. I have no idea how she found out what was happening in my family, but one day she told me that for the rest of my life I was going to be a child of divorce.

I think something that helped Ruby and me feel instantly comfortable around each other was the fact that both of us have divorced parents. Ruby's dad lives in Michigan. She visits him for a week at Christmas, an occasional long weekend from school, and two weeks in the summer. One time, when I was sleeping over at her apartment and we were whispering at night, she admitted that her dad feels more like an uncle than an actual parent. For most of the year, it's just Ruby and her mom sharing a tidy apartment with colorful bedspreads and lavender soaps and sweeping views of the Manhattan skyline.

I definitely remember my parents together, like family vacations we took to Vermont and how, when I was little, we used to snuggle on our couch and have Friday pizza-and-movie nights. Right after they split up, my dad moved out of our apartment to a rental place nearby and my mom stayed with Benji and me. Benji was only four then. But then my mom got an offer to be a history professor at a college upstate. It was her dream job. She talked about bringing Benji and me with her, but I freaked out and said I wouldn't leave New York City. Even in second grade, change and I didn't mix well, and also I was already seeing my occupational therapist, Maureen. My parents decided it was important for me to live in the city, stay at my school, and continue working with Maureen.

My dad gave up his rental place, moved back into our apartment, and became the full-time parent. My mom moved to Tomsville and we started visiting her every weekend. Two years ago, she and Bill got married. I knew she was together with him and I liked him enough but I still wasn't thrilled about getting a stepdad. I didn't want some guy living with my mom and eating meals with us and being around all the time. But it actually hasn't been that bad. I'm only there on weekends and school vacations, so I don't have to deal with it all the time. Also, Bill is kind of quiet and gives Benji and me a lot of time alone with our mom.

When Ruby and I get to I Scream, my dad is out front on a phone call. He's tall like me, and we both have curly blond hair, except his is short and mine is long. If I don't put my hair back in a ponytail or braids, it fluffs annoyingly around my face. For my birthday, Ruby gave me several headbands, the hard plastic kind that Avery wears to push back her hair from her forehead, but I couldn't keep them on for three seconds. They felt too tight behind my ears, like my skull was being pinched by torture equipment.

Dad holds up his hand and mouths *one second* before returning to his conversation. If he were a LEGO minifigure, he would have a phone in one yellow claw-shaped hand, and the other claw-shaped hand would be raised like *I'll be off this call in a second*. My dad knows he's guilty of checking his phone all the time. He's an architect who runs his own firm, which means he can take off a morning if we're home sick, but it also means he has to answer every call that comes in.

Ruby and I fist-bump my dad as we walk past him and head into I Scream. Ruby's mom is sitting on the long red bench next to the wall. She looks up from her phone and waves us over. There are a lot of middle school kids farther down the bench and at the tables in the window. They've got their overstuffed backpacks on the floor and their phones in their hands. I bet they go to Maya Angelou Middle School. That's my top choice and Ruby's too. Everyone calls it Maya A. I'm really hoping we both get in. We had to take an entrance exam in February and have good grades on our report cards and also get a teacher recommendation.

"Hey, Willa," Ruby's mom says to me. She kisses the top of Ruby's head and says, "Hi, Rubes."

"Bathroom!" Ruby shouts, slinging her soccer bag onto the floor and racing off toward the back of I Scream.

Ruby's mom laughs and rolls her eyes. She must be used to Ruby's frequent peeing. Ruby says that someday she'll get an X-ray of her bladder and prove to the world that it's tiny. Until then, we'll just have to take her word for it.

"How was your day, Willa?" Ruby's mom asks.

"Fine," I say.

"That's what Ruby always tells me too," she says, smiling.

Ruby and her mom have the same long, thick hair and straight nose but the similarities end there. Ruby is really sporty and refuses to wear dresses or jewelry while her mom is always in high heels and dresses, and she has a diamond stud on her left nostril. Ruby's mom is Indian, but she grew up in Michigan and went to law school in Connecticut. Ruby hates it when people ask her, "Where are you *really* from?" as if being Indian makes it impossible for her to be American. She always says she's from America and that's it.

"Willa wants to know why we're here," Ruby says to her mom as she returns from the bathroom and plops onto the bench. "She thinks it's about middle school but I said probably not."

When Ruby says *middle school*, I glance nervously at the Maya A. kids. They seem like giants or teenagers or teenage giants.

"Well," Ruby's mom says, glancing out onto the sidewalk where my dad is gesturing in the air, his phone pressed against his ear. "Greg and I want to talk to you girls, and we thought it would be nice to meet somewhere fun and neutral."

Greg. That's the first thing that throws me. Parents don't usually refer to other parents by their first names. They always say *your dad* or *Willa's dad*. And somewhere neutral? Bad news is coming for sure. When my parents told Benji and me that they were splitting up, they did it on a bench in Central Park because they wanted it to be "a neutral place." Even though I was seven, I still remember those exact words.

"Want to pick out your ice cream and sorbet?" Ruby's mom says, gesturing toward the soft-serve handles. "Get whatever you want and I'll meet you at the cashier to pay."

"Sure," Ruby says, slurping in some saliva. Even though she's had her palate expander for as long as I've known her, it still brings on extreme drool. "How many samples can we get?"

"Just one," Ruby's mom says. "Make sure it's lactose-free for you, Rubes. And don't forget your favorite topping."

"As if," Ruby says, starting toward the handles. "Come on, Willa. Gummy bears are calling us."

Instead of following her, I hover nervously above a red stool, kicking my feet into the floor. I haven't even taken off my backpack. I'm getting that feeling like I need to know exactly what's going on *right now* or I'm going to shriek and wiggle my hands. The thing is, I would never show that side of me in front of Ruby or in I Scream with all the middle schoolers around. I reach into my backpack for a piece of Trident and slide it into my mouth. My occupational therapist, Maureen, has taught me to always have an emergency pack of gum for times like these.

"Hey, Waggy," my dad says, walking in and tousling my hair.

I quickly move away from him and hiss, "Stop it."

I glance at Ruby's mom, who looks down at her pale-pink polished fingernails. I don't want to be rude, but *Waggy? In public?* That's been his nickname for me since I was a toddler and used to crawl around and woof like a dog. My full name is Willa Anderson Garrett, initials W.A.G. It's fitting because I love dogs. But that doesn't give him permission to go *Waggy* on me in the middle of I Scream.

"What should I call you?" he asks. "Just plain Willa?"

"Exactly," I tell him. Really, it should be obvious.

"Okay," Dad says. "Just Plain Willa it is." He slides onto the bench next to Ruby's mom and sets his phone facedown on the table.

Usually I don't mind his Dad Jokes, but I'm not in the mood right now. "Please," I say, mashing my gum. "Stop."

15

I'm starting to feel like I can't breathe. Last year, when I got that tight-throat feeling, Maureen said I needed to carve out time to relax. That's when my mom and I began doing best part worst part every night on the phone.

"Why are we here, Dad?" I ask. I tug at the bracelets on my wrist, stretching out the rubber ones and letting them snap back. "What do you need to tell us?"

Dad glances at Ruby's mom and raises his eyebrows. She nods back at him.

"Rubes, come here!" she calls. Even though Ruby's mom said to sample one flavor, I can see Ruby has two sample spoons in her hand, and she's about to ask for a third.

Ruby tosses the spoons in the trash, walks over, and flops onto the bench.

"Sit down," my dad instructs me, pointing to the stool.

Even though I'm annoyed at him, I want to hear what's coming next, so I reluctantly sit down.

"We've thought a lot about the best way to tell you girls," Dad says. "We weren't sure how you'd take it, but we're hoping you'll be happy because we think it's exciting."

"Exciting in your opinion," I mutter. I don't mean to. It just slips out. I won't let myself look at Ruby. She's never seen this side of me, the moody side, the calling-out side. That's Private Willa, only for family. Just like the fact that I go to occupational therapy twice a week. *Private*.

"What's that?" Dad asks.

"Nothing," I say.

"The thing is—" Dad starts, but then he says to Ruby's mom, "maybe this wasn't such a good idea, Sandhya."

First *Greg*. Now *Sandhya*.

"What wasn't?" I ask.

"We're here," Ruby's mom says. "We've started."

"Started what?" I ask.

"Shhhh!" Ruby says. "Let them talk already."

I wrinkle my nose at her. This isn't her business. Oh yeah. I guess it is.

"Greg and I are dating." Ruby's mom reaches over and places her hand on top of my dad's. "We've been seeing each other."

My gum slides straight down my throat in a river of saliva. *Great*. Now it's going to lurk undigested in my stomach for seven years, reminding me of this terrible moment.

Ruby squeals. "Why didn't you tell me, Mom? Like, Willa's dad is your boyfriend now?"

I shake my head slowly from side to side. I can't believe this is happening.

"We didn't want to involve you until we were sure," Ruby's mom says.

"Sure of what?" Ruby asks. She has a huge smile on her face like it's great news when the truth is that this is terrible, terrible news. The worst news ever. I stare down at my lap.

My dad smiles right back at her. "Sure we're in love."

17

I look up quickly. Only I wish I hadn't, because at that second my dad is turning his hand over and clasping Ruby's mom's fingers.

"And we are." Ruby's mom beams at my dad. "Very much so."

I grab my backpack off the floor and storm out onto the sidewalk.

CHAPTER 3

I'm pacing in front of the polka-dot awning of I Scream when Dad and Ruby's mom and Ruby come out. Ruby is my best friend but I wish she'd disappear right now. Then I would be able to cry and stomp my feet and ask my dad how on earth he could FALL IN LOVE WITH RUBY'S MOM.

For one, I didn't even know he wanted a girlfriend. I thought he was fine with Benji and me and the people at his architecture firm and the dads from Benji's parkour class. I've heard people mention setting my dad up on dates over the past few years, but he always said his hands were full with work and parenting. For two, my dad is a *boyfriend*? Boyfriends are in high school or college. They are not dads who tell Dad Jokes and clean crumbs out of lunch boxes and check hair for lice. And for three, his girlfriend is Ruby's mom? Sandhya Kapoor seems perfectly fine. She's a lawyer for an environmental agency. She's always dressed sort of fancy. She knows I don't eat meat, so once when I slept over she made us a big vegetarian meal with spinach and chickpeas, and she

19

doesn't cut off our screen time after thirty minutes the way my dad does. But that's all I know about her.

"I know this comes as a surprise," Dad says to me now. He's turning his phone over and over in his hands, which is what he does when he's nervous.

"Willa," Ruby's mom says, touching my arm. "I can tell you're upset. Let's go someplace quieter, like the diner across the street? We can get an order of fries and talk it all out."

"That sounds nice!" Dad says, forcing a smile.

I shrink away from Ruby's mom. That's the last thing I want, to be trapped in a booth, *talking it all out*. There's no *all* to talk out. I just want to be alone in my room, building my LEGO dog kingdom. Mom gave me a litter of LEGO dogs last weekend. I've connected three baseplates and now I'm constructing a kingdom for them with a castle and pens and feeding areas.

Ruby is standing next to her mom, peering curiously at me. She's never seen me like this. She's only seen me as happy Willa, silly Willa, always chattering and joking around. But that's just one side of me, the side I show in school. There's the other side, the weird side, the side I keep private.

"Can we also find a bathroom?" Ruby asks. "I have to pee again."

"Of course," her mom says. "There'll be one at the diner."

"We should actually head home," Dad says to Ruby's mom. He says it quietly, their faces way too close for my comfort. "Take some time to process this."

If Dad were a LEGO minifigure, I would snap hand-cuffs on him so he could never grasp Ruby's mom's fingers again.

Ruby's mom nods and then smiles sympathetically at me. "It's going to be okay, Willa. Promise."

I stare down at the blackened gum dots on the sidewalk. This is how much she doesn't know me.

"See you soon, Ruby," Dad says. "Maybe we can kick around a soccer ball this weekend?"

"Sure," Ruby tells him. "Sounds fun."

"But Benji and I are up at Mom's this weekend, so—" I start to say, but then I pause because it dawns on me that even though my brother and I aren't in the city on Saturdays and Sundays, Ruby and her mom are here. And now that my dad is in love with Ruby's mom, he will be seeing them even if it doesn't involve me.

No one says anything for an awkward second. I don't even smile when a dalmatian passes us and waggles his spotted tail in my direction.

"I guess we'll go to the subway," Ruby's mom finally says to my dad. "Let's talk later?"

Dad nods. He attempts to put his arm around me but I wriggle it off. I seriously do not want to be touched right now.

"Bye, Willa," Ruby says as they start walking away.

Dad nudges me. "Say good-bye to Ruby."

"Bye . . ." I call softly after her. It's not that I'm trying to be rude. I just have no idea what to say.

Ruby leans over to me and whispers in my ear, "Now you definitely have your worst part."

I smile weakly. Because even though this is awful, Ruby is a great best friend. I just don't want that, or anything else, to change.

"The thing is," Ruby adds, "this is going to be really fun. Think about how much time we'll get to spend together. Maybe we'll even become sisters!"

My face falls. I seriously might freak out right here on the sidewalk, like a full-on squeal and a wild, arm-flapping dance. My occupational therapist, Maureen, says I do this when I don't feel at home in my body and I need to scream and shake until the feeling goes away.

Ruby looks expectantly at me, waiting for me to agree with her.

Wrong! I want to say. *We have to let them know that falling in love is a terrible idea and they need to stop it immediately.* But by the time I regain the ability to talk, she's already returned to her mom, and she's clutching her hand and tugging her toward a bathroom.

....

On the walk home, Dad asks, "Do you want to talk about it?"

"No," I say flatly.

"Willa, you know it's going to be okay, right? Like

remember when Mom met Bill and it was hard at first but then it all worked out?"

"Mom and Bill is totally different than you and Ruby's mom," I snap. "Also I said I don't want to talk about it." I twist my ankles inward and walk a few steps like that. Maybe on some people this would hurt but I'm double-jointed that way.

After a few minutes, my dad starts chattering about anything and everything else. He tells me about a woman on the subway with an adorable service dog. He tells me about a guy in his architecture firm who bought himself a seven-hundred-piece LEGO set. He suggests we order veggie nachos tonight, which he knows I love more than any other food group. Usually to get him to order veggie nachos I have to complete five days of a working-hard-to-control-my-body behavior chart.

Throughout all my dad's attempts at conversation, I frown and shrug and don't say anything back.

Finally he says, "Want to do dog names? I've thought of some brand-new ones that I think you're going to love."

He knows he has me. I never say no to doing dog names. For my entire life, in addition to having W.A.G. as my initials, I've wanted a dog so much that my dad finally declared I have a dog-shaped hole in my heart. That—and a convincing phone call from Maureen, who said that a dog would help me settle my body—is what made him agree to get me a dog this summer even though he's a single parent and we live in an apartment without a yard.

"What new dog names do you have?" I ask cautiously.

Dad grins at me. "I've been thinking about breakfast foods. Sweet and yummy. Like Waffle? Or Maple? Or Biscuit?"

"Biscuit is that dog from the picture books," I say grouchily. "That would be copying. Ms. Lacey says that plagiarism could get us kicked out of middle school next year."

"Bacon?"

I groan. "I'm a vegetarian."

"Cinnamon?"

"Okay, that's cute," I have to admit.

"Cinnnn-a-mon," he calls, trying it on for size.

"It works across a park," I say, imagining a puppy barreling toward me, its pink tongue flapping. "No, it's too long. They say two syllables are better."

We stop at the corner and let an ambulance scream past, lights flashing and sirens blaring. Dad cups his hands over his ears. Sometimes I do that but other times—like now—I love the noise. Loud noises quiet my brain, which then makes my body feel calm. No one gets it when I try to explain it, but that's how it is for me. Same with hand dryers and subways pulling into the station. Mostly I love them. But other times they make me feel itchy and uncomfortable, like I need to wriggle straight out of my skin.

"How about Oatmeal?" Dad says, a teasing grin on his face. "Or Cream of Wheat?"

"Ewww!" I shriek. "You're grossing me out!"

Dad knows that foods with slimy textures make me want to barf. Seriously, if a soft brownish banana comes near me, I will heave all over the place.

"Gruel?" Dad asks, laughing. "Grits?"

The problem is, once I'm laughing along with him, things start feeling normal. But then I remember that things are *definitely* not normal because my dad has a girlfriend and it's Ruby's mom. Dad must notice the change because he slides his arm around my shoulder. This time, I let him.

"Willa," he says, giving me a tight squeeze, "I'm sorry Sandhya and I told you that way. We were excited and we thought it would be fun because we all met at I Scream and you girls love their gummy-bear toppings so much. But I know change is hard for you, and I should have told you alone, not with Ruby, so you'd have time to process it your own way."

"Have you told Benji yet?" I ask.

My dad shakes his head. "I'm going to talk to him when we get home. I'm hoping you can give us a few minutes alone. Or actually, you can be there too. That might be nice for both of you."

I quickly shake my head. No way do I want to hear the news announced *again*!

"If you want a girlfriend so badly," I say, "can't you pick someone who's not Ruby's mom? That's just weird. I don't even know what I'm going to say to her tomorrow at school."

"I wasn't looking for a girlfriend. After your mom and I . . . after the divorce, my primary focus has been you and Benji. It was only once I met Sandhya that everything changed." Dad clears his throat. "I'm not saying you and Benji aren't my primary focus now, because you still are. I'm just saying I realized I had room in my life for more. For love."

"But Ruby is my best friend. Didn't you think of *that*?"

My dad shakes his head. "Sandhya and I started dating before you became best friends. Or I suppose it all happened at the same time."

"What's that supposed to mean?" I pull away from my dad. "Ruby and I met last fall. Before school started."

"And Sandhya and I have been dating since last fall. Since we all first met."

"Hang on," I say, my voice rising. "You've been together all this time and lying to us about it?"

Dad's phone goes off. He stands there like he's not sure what to do. He never ignores his phone, but then again I've never accused him of lying. He pulls it out, glances at the screen, and then puts it back in his pocket.

"I wasn't lying, Willa. *Lying* is a strong word."

Grown-ups always say that lying is a strong word. As if we don't know that. As if because it's a strong word it means they'd never do it.

"So what would you call being in love with my best friend's mom for this entire year and not telling me?"

"What I'm trying to explain . . ." Dad starts, but then his phone goes off again and he ignores it again. "What I'm trying to explain is that when you and Ruby met at I Scream last August and hit it off, so did Sandhya and I. We got coffee soon after and, well . . . neither of us was looking for love, but that's what it became. We didn't want to tell you and Ruby and Benji until we knew it was serious. We knew it would be big news for all three of you, and a real adjustment. Also we were always aware of how it could affect your friendship, you and Ruby. We were actually going to wait until the end of the school year so you could have the summer to adjust to us being together."

"This isn't changing the fact that we're getting a dog this summer, is it?" I ask quickly.

Dad shakes his head. "Of course not. A promise is a promise. There's a little Cinnamon or Waffle or Gruel just waiting for you to adopt her."

Definitely her. Definitely a girl dog. That's my requirement. It's time to balance out the girl-boy ratio in our house.

"Not Gruel," I say.

Dad laughs, but I'm serious. I'm not in a laughing mood right now.

We're almost at our building when I turn to Dad.

"So why did you tell us now? You said you were going to wait until the end of the school year."

"That's the thing," Dad says. He's frowning and his blondish eyebrows are thatched tight.

"*What* thing?"

"Some people from your school found out."

My arms prickle with goose bumps. "What people? Who? Ms. Lacey?"

Dad clears his throat. "You know that girl, the one who's always driving you crazy?"

"Please don't tell me that Avery Tanaka knows about you and Ruby's mom!" I say, my voice rising in horror. If Avery knows, my life is officially over.

"Sandhya and I went out to dinner last night," Dad says. "We were at an Italian restaurant near Columbus Circle."

"I thought you had dinner with work people," I say. Our sitter, Joshua, stayed late yesterday, and we had penne pasta with butter and celery sticks and played thirty minutes of Minecraft. But that's not unusual. Joshua usually stays late once or twice a week.

"I don't always have dinner with work people," Dad says. "Sometimes I meet up with friends."

Or girlfriends, I think in my head. Ugh. Barf.

"We were walking out of the restaurant when we ran into the Tanaka family. Avery and her sister and her parents. Her parents are actually very nice."

Of course the Tanakas were all together. Avery has a perfect family with her perfect sister and her perfect dog and her still-married parents.

"But how did they know?" I ask. "You and Ruby's mom could have been having dinner to talk about parent stuff. Or middle schools. Or . . . whatever!"

Dad clears his throat. "We were holding hands."

"Did you say anything to them?"

"We didn't have to. They said congratulations and asked how long we've been together. We asked them to keep it private. We said that none of our kids knew yet."

I remember that smirk Avery gave us after school. I remember how her mom grimaced at us from across the street. This is suddenly much worse than I ever could have imagined possible.

"Avery didn't say anything to you today, did she?" Dad asks. "Sandhya and I were very clear that—"

I break ahead and run up the sidewalk and into our building. Instead of taking the elevator to the sixth floor, where we live, I run up the stairs. It feels good to pound the steps, to get some anger out of my legs. I want to make it to the apartment before my dad, let myself in, and hide away in my room. But when I get to the front door, I dig around in my backpack for my keys and all I feel are gum wrappers and a half-eaten granola bar. I must have forgotten my keys this morning because I was so busy listening to Dad tell me about the I Scream plan. If only I'd said, *Sorry . . . no thanks on meeting up today . . . gummy bears on ice cream aren't so great after all*.

I press my back against the wall in our hallway and slide

down until I'm slumped on the floor, my head between my knees, waiting for my dad to get off the elevator and let me into the apartment.

This is why I don't like surprises. There's no place to put them, no way for them to feel normal in my body. But everybody expects you to deal with surprises. No, everyone expects you to be *excited* about them, like how Ruby squealed and smiled when they dumped the news on us.

Well, I'm not excited. Sorry.

My occupational therapist has a shirt that says, SORRY I'M DIFFERENT. SORRY NOT SORRY. That's how I feel right now. Sorry not sorry.

CHAPTER 4

"Willa?" my mom says when I answer her call.
She and I always talk on the iPad but we only do audio
because Mom says I can't focus on a call when I stare at my
face in the corner of the screen. I keep the iPad in my room
so I can call her whenever I want or she can call me without
going through my dad's cell. If she's not teaching a class, we
often call for a check-in when I get home from school.

"Daddy texted me that you're upset," Mom says. "He
said you might want to talk."

I snap a red LEGO brick onto a baseplate to start building a flower box on one side of the dog run, and then I dig
through my bin for stray flower pieces.

"I hear LEGOs," Mom says. "Are you in your room?"

"Yeah. I'm working on my dog kingdom."

To call it a room is a stretch. It's more like a Girl Cave.
Officially, our apartment is a three-bedroom, but two of
the bedrooms are huge, and then we have a small side room

where we used to dump winter clothes and old toys. Until last year, Benji and I shared one of the big rooms with twin beds and dressers and shelves with books and LEGOs and binders of Pokémon cards. But then we started bickering because Benji said I'm messy and I said he talks too much about history and geography. I swear, living with Benji is like living with Google. My dad proposed the idea of one of us taking over the little room and I was like, *me, me, me*! I love being in tight spaces, like back seats of cars and refrigerator boxes. My Girl Cave can only fit a bed, a small dresser, and a mat for LEGO building, but it's snug and cozy and perfect for me. One of my favorite parts is my big poster of a golden retriever by the door.

"Honey," Mom says as I click the flower pieces onto the stems, "we were concerned you'd be upset about this news, but I think it could be exciting for you and Benji. Think about how it was an adjustment when I married Bill—but then it's all gone so well."

"Bill is not Ruby's mom!" I shout. Why is everyone assuming these are similar situations? Because they're not. Not even a little bit.

"That's true," Mom says, "but—"

"Hang on," I say, cutting her off. I tug at the sock on my left foot, the same one that was driving me crazy as Ruby and I were walking to I Scream. Now there's a crinkle poking into my toes. My dad pre-wore my socks for me this morning, getting them good and stretched out, so I don't know why this one is bothering me now. "How long have you known about this and not told me?"

My mom sighs. "Daddy and I talk, Willa."

"You didn't answer me," I say. This sock is driving me crazy! My mom buys my socks from a special website for kids with sensory issues. None of their clothes are supposed to have seams or tags or crinkles. I pull off the sock and throw it under my bed. Hopefully I won't see it again until next year or maybe never.

"Honey," Mom says, "I've known for a while but I respected their desire to keep it private. Daddy and I talk about all the things in our lives that are relevant to you and Benji. That's what it means to co-parent, honey. We always want to make sure—"

"Why are you saying *honey* so much?" I snap, cutting her off. "Are you trying to make it better? Because Dad and Ruby's mom together is awful and weird and gross. I thought at least you'd take my side on this. Did you know that Avery Tanaka already found out?"

"I'm not taking sides," Mom says, "because there aren't sides to take. Bill and I are happy together. Daddy deserves a good relationship too."

Now my other sock is poking into my toes. I peel it off and chuck it under the bed.

"Where did you get these socks?" I say. "I thought they didn't have seams! And did you hear what I said about Avery?"

33

"What socks?" Mom asks.

"The green ones with the white stripes. I thought they were from that special website. I can't believe Avery knows about Dad and Ruby's mom. She's going to torture me."

Mom sighs again. I'm making everyone sigh today. Whatever. Let them sigh.

"Bring up the socks this weekend and I'll mail them back," she says. "And Avery isn't going to torture you. She's a person too. She probably just wants to be friends with you and doesn't know how. I've always thought that about Avery, like how you both love dogs. She's probably jealous of how easily you make friends. And if she gives you a hard time, talk to Ms. Lacey."

For a college professor, Mom isn't acting very smart. Seriously. Avery wants to be *friends* with me? More like she wants to make sure I'm miserable on a daily basis. Also, Avery is mean in a sneaky way that teachers never see. Whenever an adult is around, she smiles and they think she's as sweet as cotton candy. Which I happen to hate. Too sticky on my fingers.

"Is Daddy nearby?" Mom says. "Can you put him on?"

"I think he's in the middle of telling Benji the bad news," I say.

Mom pauses. I can tell she's annoyed, but she's hardly in a position to chew me out. She says she loves me and that she'll call me again tonight. I mumble good-bye and shove my iPad under a heap of clothes.

After a few minutes, I push my LEGOs aside and wriggle into my body sock, which Mom ordered for me from another sensory website. It's like a sleeping bag except it's made from a thin, stretchy material. When I'm in it, it squeezes my body and I feel snug and safe. Unlike most of the time when I feel like a kite being jerked around by gusts and occasional hurricane-speed winds.

Maureen, my occupational therapist, says that's part of having Sensory Processing Disorder. It's hard to explain Sensory Processing Disorder—I guess it means that it's harder for me to be a person in the world than it is for most people. Like how I hate slimy textures and the taste of eggs makes me gag and I can never wear shirts with tight collars or jeans that squeeze my knees. I hate bright overhead lights, and having my toenails trimmed makes me howl in pain. And don't even talk to me about perfume. Total chemical overload. But, at the same time, I love being squeezed by a body sock and I can't get enough of certain tastes, like passion fruit. I could taste passion fruit forever. Beyond touch and taste and smell issues, it's also hard for me to control my energy level, and I'm kind of clumsy and I'm always losing things. Water bottles are the worst. I lose my water bottle every few weeks.

My mom says she first noticed something was different about me when I was a toddler and she took me to a Music Together class. While the other kids danced in a circle and shook their plastic gourds, I hid in a corner of the gym and beat a drum until long after the song was over. And then there were other things. I kept falling onto the sidewalk and chipping my baby teeth. And I couldn't climb out of the sandbox like all the other kids. And even though I hated my music class, I loved pounding pots and pans and making my own noise.

That's why Sensory Processing Disorder is hard to explain. It's different in every person. For me, I hate some textures and love others. Like I love nachos and popcorn because they're awesome to crunch. But I can't stand the crunch of a baby carrot. I can chew a baby carrot for ten minutes and still have a mouthful of orange gunk. Sometimes I hate crowds and other times I love being surrounded by people. And my shins? Covered in bruises. I'm not chipping teeth anymore but I'm still clumsy.

When I was four, I started going to occupational therapy. For a few years, I also saw a physical therapist who taught me how to jump and climb, and I had appointments with a speech therapist who gave me bumpy plastic toys to chew. I even had a special teacher following me around in preschool, telling me not to hug other children so hard they'd topple over. I doubt I ever hugged Avery Tanaka back in preschool, but my mom told me that once at pickup I tried to bite her sweatshirt.

Yeah, I was a weird kid.

I'm still weird now, but it's more Invisible Weird. I no longer knock over my classmates or bite their sweatshirts, and I've gotten strong enough to climb ladders like anyone else. No one at school even knows I have Sensory Processing Disorder. But that doesn't mean it's not there. I still have my tagless clothes and my leggings that aren't too tight and aren't too loose, and my dad is always making me charts and giving me rewards for filling up the charts. I get stickers for controlling my body or keeping my thoughts in my thought bubble. For my current chart, I have to fill forty squares and then my dad is going to buy me a mini-trampoline just like the one Maureen has in her sensory gym. I already have twenty-seven stickers, which means he could be ordering it in the next few weeks!

I still see Maureen every Monday and Wednesday afternoon. I never tell anyone at school because seeing an occupational therapist sounds weird. Whenever someone asks where I'm going, I just say I have a math tutor. I'd rather have people think I struggle with math than know I struggle with being Willa.

....

Forty minutes later, the buzzer rings and my little brother, Benji, shouts, "Noche Mexicana is here!"

Even though I said I'm never coming out of my room, I'm also really hungry. The last thing I ate was a few bites of my bagel sandwich at lunch because my friend Zoe was slurping a yogurt squeeze across from me when a creamy pink dribble slid down her chin and that was the end of my appetite.

"Noche Mexicana!" Benji shouts again. I can hear him jumping from the side of the couch, kicking off a wall, and then lunging onto a chair. Benji says that if he wants to get on the show *American Ninja Warrior* someday then he needs to practice his parkour nonstop for the next decade.

I curl up tighter in my body sock and consider how mad I am at my dad versus how much I love veggie nachos. Also I thought he was going to tell Benji the bad news as soon as we got home, but judging by my brother's jumping and lunging he seems like his regular happy self. Which means—*oh no*—maybe Dad is waiting to tell Benji about him and Ruby's mom during dinner tonight. Which means I'm never coming out of my room for sure. Then again, when I get the image of nachos in my brain I really can't think about anything else until I've eaten a big platter of them.

Dad must be reading my mind because he says, "I'm currently unpacking two burritos and one order of veggie nachos hold the sour cream, hold the mushrooms, extra cheese, extra guacamole on the side."

He knows that's how I like my nachos. Sour cream is too yogurty and mushrooms are fungi that grow on tree stumps. I love that Noche Mexicana is good about holding those ingredients, and also they blend their guacamole so there aren't any slimy avocado chunks that make me want to barf.

"Noche Mexicana, Willa!" Benji shouts for a third time. "Come eat your nachos before I do!"

My brother is three years and a month younger than me.

Other than the fact that he thinks I'm messy and I think he talks too much, we generally get along. That said, I don't trust him to leave my nachos alone. I wiggle out of my body sock, kick it to the floor, and make my way to the table. Dad and Benji are already sitting down, tinfoil mounds of steak burritos on their plates and napkins in their laps. I slide into my seat, eying Benji carefully to try to figure out what he knows. He's busy unwrapping his burrito, though, and doesn't look up at me.

"Napkin in your lap," Dad says to me out of habit. Every meal I forget and every meal he has to remind me. I don't get the whole napkin-in-your-lap thing, because mainly you need your napkin for wiping your face and hands. Just like why do you have to make your bed in the morning if you're going to crawl back in at night? Pointless.

"I told Benji about Sandhya and me a few minutes ago," Dad says, "and he knows that I told you after school today."

My hand freezes midway into my mouth. I was warming up with a simple bite, one chip with a smudge of beans. After that I go for the grandmama bites, which are multiple chips heaped with beans, melted cheese, guacamole, salsa, and caramelized onions.

I stare hard at Benji and mouth *No!* across the table. My brother has roundish brown eyes and soft brown hair, and he's really smart. Like he knows more about history and geography than most high school students. I'm hoping that if Benji says that our dad and Ruby's mom together is a terrible idea, it will make Dad reconsider. At least Benji could have a decent meltdown and cry and make Dad see that both his kids are miserable with this new girlfriend business.

But instead of backing me up in any way, Benji shrugs and says, "Whatever. It's a free country."

"How can you say that?" I ask, shoving a grandmama bite into my mouth but not even tasting it.

"It's no big deal, Willa," Benji says. "Dad has a girlfriend and it's Ruby's mom. As long as they don't start kissing all the time, it's fine with me."

"Did you hear about Avery?" I ask. "She knows. She saw them together."

Benji shrugs and leans into his burrito. Just then, Dad's phone rings. He touches the screen and quickly says, "I'll call you back." I wonder if it's Ruby's mom. Dad and Ruby's mom are probably going to whisper into their phones later about how badly I'm handling the news and how wonderfully Benji and Ruby are doing with it.

"Sandhya is Indian, right?" Benji asks.

"She was born in Mumbai," Dad says. "Her family moved to Michigan when she was five. But her parents have retired and moved back."

Ruby has mentioned her grandparents in India. She told me that every other summer she and her mom visit them. It's a sixteen-hour flight with stopovers in places like Amsterdam and Dubai.

"Mumbai used to be Bombay," Benji says. "They changed the name in 1995."

Benji has always been this way. Last year he memorized everything about all the US presidents. The year before that it was capital cities. This spring he's been reading the world atlas and cross-referencing it with the encyclopedia and books about foreign currencies. The thing about Benji is that even though he's brainy, he's also athletic and has lots of friends. He's the perfect combination of my mom, who is a history professor, and my dad, who is outgoing and into sports and doesn't sweat the small stuff. I prefer fiction to history and *anything* to sports. I have some friends but not a ton. And I totally sweat the small stuff.

Dad's phone rings again.

As Dad glances at the screen, Benji says to me, "Do you think it's Sandhya calling to blow kisses into the phone?" Then my brother cracks up so hard at his non-joke that he has to guzzle a bunch of water to stop coughing.

I roll my eyes. First Ruby. Now Benji. Everyone is acting like Dad's news is no big deal, like it's exciting, like it's even funny.

But I can't do that. No way.

CHAPTER 5

It takes me forever to get dressed for school the next morning. Not because I care about fashion like some fifth graders I know. Mostly I dress to be comfortable, and today *nothing* feels good. I yank off all my leggings and my loose cotton pants, and I beg my dad to let me wear shorts even though the high today is only fifty-four degrees. Finally he comes into my room and digs through my drawers looking for leggings that will work. I'm crying hard by the time he agrees to let me wear my longest shorts. I have to promise to keep on my sweatshirt all day so at least my top half is warm.

As we're walking out of our building, Dad says he's ready to take a nap. Benji tells him that Winston Churchill spent a good portion of every workday in his bed. I point out a Cavalier King Charles spaniel on the sidewalk and then try not to think about Cavalier King Charles spaniels, because that's the kind of dog that Avery owns, and I don't want to think about how Avery is going to rub in my terrible news at school today.

On the walk to The Children's School, Dad and Benji talk about parkour and ninja training. My brother loves watching shows where people compete in obstacle courses using extreme climbing and gymnastics. Sometimes I watch with him even though there's no way I'll ever have the strength to sprint straight up a warped wall. My dad's real passion is soccer, but since Benji is obsessed with being a ninja, Dad is getting into it too. He signed Benji up for climbing on Thursdays, and he's assistant coaching his Saturday morning parkour class in Riverside Park.

As we get closer to school, I say good-bye to Dad and run ahead into the building. We often bump into Ruby and her mom at drop-off and that could be a major problem today. Like, what if my dad and Ruby's mom decide that now that they've told us the news they can start kissing and hugging every morning? Thinking about that, I run through the lobby of school and up all five flights of stairs. I'm breathing hard as I stumble into Ms. Lacey's classroom and fling my backpack onto a hook by the door.

"Hey, Willa," Ruby says.

As soon as I see her, my stomach jumps around nervously. She's the only one in the classroom so far, except for Ms. Lacey, who is over at her desk reading her phone and wiping her nose with a tissue. Our teacher says she's counting the seconds until the trees stop blossoming.

"Hey," I say to Ruby. I wonder if she also came in early to avoid any possible parental kissing and hugging. Like, maybe she's come to her senses that her mom and my dad being together is weird and gross.

"Why are you here early?" I ask hopefully.

"My mom had to be in court for a trial this morning, so she dropped me off ten minutes ago," Ruby says.

"Oh," I reply flatly.

"I couldn't stop thinking about it all night," Ruby says, smiling. "Can you believe it? Think about how much fun we're going to have."

"Shut up!" I snap.

Ms. Lacey looks up from her phone, sniffles, and touches her finger to her lips. I know I can be loud without realizing it, but what Ms. Lacey doesn't understand is that this is no time to be a quiet and calm type of person. This is the time to shut Ruby up before she broadcasts to the whole world that my dad has a girlfriend, and it's her mom.

"Jeez, Willa." Ruby shakes her head. "I didn't even say anything."

"I'm sorry," I say quickly. The last thing I want is to be in a fight with Ruby on top of everything else. "It's just . . . it's not like I want to tell everyone."

"Like who?" Ruby says, looking around. "No one is even here. Honestly, Willa, it's going to be awesome. I'm so glad that of all the people they could have picked—"

"Can we please not talk about it?" I tug at my shorts, trying to inch them down toward my knees. Even though most days I like my legs liberated from pants, my skin is feeling cold and shivery right now, and all I want is to be wrapped in warm fabric.

Ruby pushes her tongue up into her palate expander and then sucks in some saliva. "Okay . . . but before everyone gets here I just wanted to say that your dad is really nice. And funny. So I'm happy for my mom."

Now is when I'm supposed to say that Ruby's mom is also really nice. And she *is* nice. But being nice does *not* mean I want her to be my dad's girlfriend.

"Did you hear about Avery?" I ask, changing the subject.

Ruby visibly shudders. "Okay, *that* was annoying. They did *not* need to hold hands in front of the Tanakas. They should have just kept their business to themselves."

"So you don't want everyone to know?" I ask hopefully.

Ruby shakes her head. "*Everyone* is fine. Just not Avery. Avery will find a way to make it seem bad."

For a second, I'm glad there's something Ruby and I agree on. But as I tip back and forth in my chair, I realize that Ruby said that Avery will *find a way* to make it bad. The thing is, Avery doesn't have to *find a way* to make it bad. It IS already bad.

When Avery walks into the classroom a few minutes later, I rock so vigorously in my chair I end up crashing backward into a bookshelf, knocking two science books and a row of novels onto the floor. Thank goodness Ms. Lacey is in the hallway, because if you're too disruptive she'll make you sit in the Think Chair, which is a beanbag chair at the

45

edge of the classroom where people go when they have to chill out. It's humiliating to do time in the Think Chair, because everyone glances at you while you pretend not to notice.

As I quickly shove the books back onto the shelf, I try not to look at Avery. She's wearing a black dress and a white plastic headband with black glitter and black-and-white sparkly earrings. Teachers love Avery, but I can see through the sparkles and glitter to her evil core. I settle back at my table and glance over at Ruby, who is flipping a page in her book. We're all supposed to read quietly before morning meeting. I'm reading *Because of Winn-Dixie* for the fourth time. Girl saves dog, dog saves girl—it doesn't get better than that. But I can't concentrate on a single word right now.

"Aren't you cold, Willa?" Avery asks, fiddling with the charm bracelet on her wrist as she peers at my shorts. "It was in the forties this morning."

"I'm fine," I say, tugging my shorts farther down over my knees.

"Just say it, Avery," Ruby says coolly. "We know you saw them on Wednesday night."

Ruby doesn't get nervous around Avery like I do. Probably because she hasn't known Avery since preschool and hasn't been subjected to as much torture at her manicured fingertips.

"Yes, I saw them," Avery says. "And, Willa, you probably know that your dad texted my mom last night and said that they told you guys. You have no idea how hard it was to keep it a secret all day yesterday."

Ruby glances at me worriedly but I'm holding my breath, waiting to see where Avery is going with this.

"Don't worry," Avery says. "My mom said I'm not supposed to tell people about it. She said it's your business."

I exhale slowly. This actually isn't as terrible as I anticipated.

Avery clicks a dog charm against a silver *A* on her bracelet. "Since no one else is around, I guess I can say one thing." She grins slyly and pauses for emphasis. "I was just thinking about how you're practically sisters now."

I can feel blood pounding in my ears. "We're not sisters!" I shout.

Ms. Lacey returns to the classroom, her red-rimmed eyes watching us closely.

Avery shrugs. "I guess I shouldn't have said 'sisters.' I should have said '*step*sisters.'"

Ruby groans. I sag back in my chair, but I'm careful to keep both feet on the ground so I don't go crashing backward again. The twins, Norie and Zoe, are looking on curiously from the next table, their books open in front of them. Along with Ruby, Norie and Zoe are my other friends in the class. Sometimes I chat with the boys, like Elijah and Sam, who live to trade LEGOs, and sometimes I even trade minifigures with them. I can see a bunch of the LEGO-trading boys watching too. *Great*. Before the end of the day everyone is going to know that my dad fell in love with my best friend's mom. Which is so weird when all I want in my life is not to be weird.

"Here's the thing," Avery says. "My sister is taking a psychology class this semester. She goes to a very selective high school."

Ruby and I shake our heads like we don't care about Avery's sister's high school, but that doesn't stop Avery. Nothing stops her from her bragging. We all know that she rocked her audition to a performing arts middle school, and her parents are rich, and her dog, Pippin, descends from a Best in Show Cavalier King Charles spaniel.

"Anyway, my sister is taking a psychology class on family relationships, and she learned that most second marriages have little chance of succeeding if there are stepchildren in the picture. I just thought you should know that. This relationship may be a short-lived problem."

"Can you just shut up?" I hiss, leaning in close to Avery. I hate to think about her and her sister talking about us.

"It's not a problem," Ruby says, sucking at her palate expander. "And what would be so wrong with being step—"

"Stop it!" I shout, jumping to my feet. My chair clatters backward onto the floor, so no doubt everyone is looking at me. Well, I don't care because right now I need them both to *stop talking*.

"Girls."

Ms. Lacey is standing between Avery and me.

"I didn't do anything!" I say. It's only now that I realize my hands are trembling.

"For real," Ruby tells Ms. Lacey. "Willa didn't do anything. Avery was—"

Ms. Lacey holds up her palm. Her eyes are watery and she's clutching a fistful of tissues. "Avery, please go to your table spot. Ruby, you can sit down again. Willa, can I please talk to you in the hallway?"

Oh god. I'm totally getting sentenced to the Think Chair.

"But I . . ." I say, wiggling my fingers. I'm trying to remember what Maureen tells me to do when I'm having sensory overload, but I can't think because my brain is crashing like an ocean during a storm.

"Ms. Lacey," Avery says, smiling sweetly, "did you know my mom is an immunologist? If you need someone to talk to about your seasonal allergies, I'm sure she would—"

"I do know that about your mom," Ms. Lacey interrupts, "but I have my own immunologist I'm working with. Now, please sit down and get your book out." Then she turns to me. "Willa," she says, her voice so nasal it comes out more like *Villa*. "Let's talk in the hallway."

My body feels jittery and I'm rolling my ankles inside and out. I can't believe *I'm* getting in trouble over this! Avery was the one who started it, and she gets to sit there smirking in her perfect headband and perfect dress. Sometimes I wish I were four years old again because I would like to go in for another bite, only this time I wouldn't stop at Avery's sweatshirt.

"Class," Ms. Lacey says, clapping her hands together. "I'm going to step out for a moment. I expect that all of you will continue reading quietly."

As everyone stares at me, I snap at a rubber band on my wrist and rock back and forth on my feet.

"Want to do a few wall pushes before we talk?" Ms. Lacey asks when we get out to the hallway. She knows I have sensory issues and will sometimes suggest wall pushes or jumping jacks in the hallway. Or she'll ask me to deliver the attendance sheet to the upstairs office. I appreciate that Ms. Lacey isn't obvious about my special needs. She always pulls me aside and tells me privately.

"No thanks," I say, tapping my fingers together. "Can you just tell me if I'm getting in trouble?"

"It seems like you're having a tough morning . . . but don't worry," Ms. Lacey says, blowing her nose. "It's a good thing I'm going to tell you."

"Good?"

Ms. Lacey smiles. "I just opened a letter from the guidance counselor." She gestures to a paper that I hadn't even realized was in her hand. "There's a kindergartner who he thinks might need your help."

The Children's School is big on having older kids work with younger kids, as reading buddies or math mentors.

"Why me?" I ask.

"She's having a hard time fitting in socially."

Oh, great. They're pairing me with the kindergarten outcast. That must be how they see me, a fifth-grade outcast mentor.

Ms. Lacey continues. "Her name is Sophie. We were talking about her the other day, and Mr. Torres told me that all she wants to do is play LEGOs. He has a big box of them and has been having her come into his office once a week to play and talk. Except she's not talking. I remembered your research paper on LEGOs, and I suggested that you play LEGOs with her. Sophie may even be inspired by you. Mr. Torres loved the idea and dropped a letter on my desk firming it up. So . . . what do you think?"

I shrug. I'll never say no to LEGOs, even if it means hanging out with a kindergartner. "What would I miss? Would I have to make up a class?"

Ms. Lacey winces like she's about to deliver bad news. "Gym. Is that okay? I know some of you wait all week for gym class."

I try to play it cool but inside I'm donkey kicking all over the place. Getting out of gym to build LEGOs! I would get out of gym to clean toilets. Okay, maybe not toilets. But I would get out of gym to replace paper towels in the bathroom. Though I might be tempted to wad up wet ones and stick them to the ceiling so they'd fall whenever Avery came in to pee.

"Sure, I'll do it," I tell Ms. Lacey.

51

The rest of the day isn't bad. Ruby and I sit together at lunch but we definitely don't talk about our parents. She's reading a book on ghosts, so we take turns telling each other scary stories. I tell Ruby a story about a doll who holds up a finger every time she kills someone. It's so creepy that Ruby has to run out of the cafeteria and into the bathroom before she wets her pants.

Other than to tell us that she has stories even creepier than ours, Avery leaves us alone at lunch. She's working on a project with the twins, Norie and Zoe Robbins. I think they're writing a pop song together. Norie and Zoe are famous at school for three reasons. For one, they're completely identical except Norie has a thin scar above her lip. For two, they get along with everyone. And for three, they're boy crazy. I don't have crushes yet, and neither does Ruby, but it's still fun to hang out with the twins.

As I'm leaving school to walk home, I pass Ruby sitting on the front steps, her elbows resting on her knees.

"Don't you have afterschool?" I ask, standing above her.

Ruby shakes her head. "My mom's picking me up soon. I'm getting my palate expander checked. If everything looks good, I'll get it off next week."

"That's great," I say. Ruby's always complaining about how food gets stuck under it and she still can't swallow her spit even after a year of having it on.

"I can't wait," Ruby says, digging her phone out of her backpack and glancing at the screen. "I'll finally be able to eat gummy bears without lying to my orthodontist."

At the mention of gummy bears, I think about I Scream yesterday. Ruby must be thinking it, too, because she sighs heavily. She picks up her soccer backpack and flops it onto her other side to make room for me. I lower myself onto the stairs and reach into my bag for a piece of gum.

"I'm sorry I told you to shut up this morning," I say, folding a stick into my mouth and vowing not to swallow this one.

"It's okay." Ruby glances at her phone again. Her cheeks are flushed, though, and she's squinting like she's upset.

"Also . . ." I pause. I'm not sure where I'm going with this but I want to say something to make Ruby look less sad. "I was thinking about it and—"

"You're excited?" Ruby asks, smiling hopefully. "Please say you're excited. I mean, think about it. We're going to have so much fun. Like maybe we'll take vacations together and do holidays and road trips. We can even have family game nights!"

"Uhhh," I say, shaking my head. The thing is, I already have a family for vacations and holidays and road trips and game nights, and I really don't want that to change. Also I like that my family is my safe place where I can be myself and never worry about looking weird.

"I was just going to say that your mom is nice," I finally tell her.

Ruby stares at me like, *Huh?*

"You said this morning that my dad is nice," I explain. "Your mom is nice too."

"Oh," Ruby says.

I sigh heavily and lean into Ruby's shoulder. She leans back and we press hard into each other. The front steps of school are crowded with kids shouting and texting their parents, but right now I feel like it's just Ruby and me. From the outside, we look so different. Ruby is small and Indian American, with her black hair and her backpack that's built to hold a soccer ball and cleats. I'm tall and white, with my curly blond hair and my Lands' End backpack full of novels and embroidered with a brown dog and my W.A.G. initials. But we don't have to look alike to be best friends.

Ruby pushes harder at my shoulder, seeing if she can tip me over. I push her back. We're both giggling and pushing into each other until we're laughing and gulping for air.

Ruby's phone pings in her hand. She glances at the screen. "Oh! My mom is almost here."

The thing is, even though Ruby's mom is nice, she's no longer just Ruby's mom. She's also my dad's girlfriend, and I totally don't want to be around when she shows up.

"Bye!" I say to Ruby, hopping up and grabbing for my backpack. "See you Monday."

54

Ruby lifts her eyebrows like she's surprised I'm rushing off so quickly. "Okay," she says. "Have a good weekend."

I suddenly remember that my dad and Ruby might play soccer together this weekend. *Ugh.* I slide another piece of gum into my mouth and hurry toward Broadway without turning back.

CHAPTER 6

Every Saturday morning, after my dad and Benji finish their parkour class in Riverside Park, we get in the car and drive to my mom's house in Tomsville. My brother and I stay there until Sunday evening, when Mom and Bill drive us back to the city after dinner. It's a two-hour drive up the Hudson River to Tomsville. Dad, Benji, and I generally chat or listen to an audio book, because my brother gets carsick from reading in the back seat. And he doesn't get just a little carsick. He's a projectile puker.

This morning as we're driving, I'm looking out the window at the blossoming trees, which makes me think about Ms. Lacey and her allergies. I yawn and stretch. That's when I notice that my brother is shuffling his Pokémon cards in his lap.

"Stop looking at those," I tell him. "It's going to make you puke."

"Benji." Dad glances into the rearview mirror. "Are you reading?"

My brother raises and lowers his narrow shoulders. "It depends on the definition of reading. Mostly I was just glancing at my cards."

"If you puke—" I start to say.

Dad's phone rings. He puts the call on speaker and says, "Hey, you."

"Hey, love," says a voice. Ruby's mom's voice.

I wrinkle my nose and look over at Benji. He's intently watching Dad. I wonder if maybe he's not as okay with the news as he acted the other night.

"You're on speaker," Dad says quickly. "I'm driving the kids up to Ellen's."

Ellen is my mom. It feels strange hearing my dad say her name to Ruby's mom, like we're all one big happy family. Which we're not.

"Oh!" Ruby's mom says, laughing. "Hi, Willa! Hi, Benji!"

Benji says, "Hey, Sandhya."

I mumble out a greeting.

My dad says he'll call her back on the drive home.

As soon as he hangs up, there's silence in the car. I'm half expecting Dad to apologize or to promise we'll order veggie nachos every night next week. But before he can say anything, Benji asks, "What was up with 'hi, love'?"

"Yeah," I say, glad to have my brother coming over to my side of things. "Are you guys going to be completely gross now?"

Dad clears his throat. "As I explained on Thursday, Sandhya and I love—"

Before he can finish, Benji goes totally second grade on him. "Dad and Sandhya sitting in a tree, K-I-S-S-I-N-G!" he sings.

"Benji, stop!" I shout. I have to admit I'm disappointed. I thought Benji was upset, but really he was just revving up for more kissing jokes.

"Benji," Dad says in a warning tone.

But Benji is steamrolling through the chant. I cover my ears for what's coming next, but my brother is singing so loud it's hard to miss.

"First comes love, then comes marriage, then comes a baby in a baby carriage!"

"Thanks for the song, Benji," Dad says. I can tell he's forcing himself to sound cheerful. "But can we please pass on any encores?"

Benji leans toward the front, stretching his seat belt as far as it will go. "You and Sandhya aren't getting married or having babies, are you?"

The car swerves slightly to the right. Dad adjusts his hands on the wheel and says, "No babies. I have you guys and she has Ruby. You're plenty."

"Good," Benji says. "Because you're a geezer."

I snort loudly.

"Thanks a lot, Benji," Dad says, glancing quickly over his

shoulder, "but are you forgetting who exercised with you and ten other eight-year-olds for an hour this morning?"

"You're not always a geezer," Benji says. "You're just too much of a geezer to have a baby."

Dad and Benji laugh, but I'm stone-cold silent. Because I just realized that when Benji asked my dad about marriage and babies, he only said no to the baby part.

"Ready?" Mom asks. She sets two plastic cups of passion fruit juice on the patio table and pulls up a chair next to the hammock.

It's Sunday morning. I love reading in the hammock in my mom's backyard, with the birds chirping and the wind tickling the leaves. My mom got this hammock for me last year. It's made from a million colorful embroidery threads, and it surrounds my body like a cocoon. My stepdad tied a rope to a nearby tree so that I can pull myself back and forth. Glancing at my mom, I lay *Because of Winn-Dixie* across my chest and yank on the rope to make the hammock swing faster.

"Ready for what?" I ask.

"To talk," she says. "Remember when you were falling asleep last night?"

Oh yeah. *That.*

Last night, when my mom came in to kiss me good-night, I kept wiggling my legs and flopping like a fish out of water because my nightgown was too hot and my pillow was too itchy. Even after I changed into a different nightgown and my mom switched my pillowcase, I couldn't settle down. Finally she placed her palms on my back and pressed down, holding me in place. That's what she used to do when I was little and couldn't control my body. After a while I must have fallen asleep.

"I haven't seen you that uncomfortable in years," Mom adds. "I'm guessing it's about Daddy and Sandhya?"

I push up from the hammock and take a sip of passion fruit juice.

"I remember you were upset when Bill and I got married and bought this house. Remember how we talked a lot about how some things would change but other things would stay the same? It took a while but . . . it's not bad, right? I think we've all adjusted."

I set down my juice and wiggle deep into the hammock. "It's different with Bill."

"I realize he's not the parent of a friend of yours," Mom says. "I know that's feeling really hard."

I roll away in the hammock. *Really hard* doesn't even begin to describe it. I feel like there's screeching in my ears and tags searing my skin and socks rubbing my toes. All at once. All the time.

"Why don't we start with best part worst part," Mom says, drinking some of her juice and setting it on the table.

I turn back to her. There's something about Mom's voice that always feels calming to me, even when I'm upset. She has the same wispy brown hair and brown eyes as Benji, except she wears glasses. Her eyes are so bad that she even needs glasses when she brushes her teeth. She complains about her vision, but I can't picture her without glasses. Plus it fits her professor personality. My mom teaches modern European history and is always surrounded by books on wars and economic crises.

"Best part," my mom says, leaning back in her chair, "is having you and Benji here. Worst part, it's Sunday, and that means you have to leave. I love teaching on Mondays, but I also feel sad when the week starts."

I wrap the hammock tighter around me. "Where is Benji anyway?"

"He's at the park with Bill, trying out the new climbing wall."

My stepdad never had kids of his own, so whenever Benji and I are here he lives out his dad fantasies with us. Bill bikes with us to a nearby park to climb on playground equipment, and he drives me to the library or the dog run to check out breeds. Benji calls him Bonus Dad. I don't go that far, but Mom's right that I've gotten okay with having Bill around. I think a big part of it is that I don't live with them full-time. Even when I hated the idea of Bill, he was just a weekend problem.

"When are Bill and Benji getting back?" I ask.

"Noon."

"What are we having for lunch?"

"Probably grilled cheese or noodles."

"Can we have noodles?"

"Honey," Mom says, pushing the hammock so I sway back and forth.

"Yeah?"

"I get the sense you're trying to avoid the subject."

I tug hard at the rope. "I just don't get it," I mutter.

"Get what?"

"Why Dad had to pick Ruby's mom. Why couldn't he have picked someone I don't know? Or stayed single? Everything was going along fine."

Mom is quiet for a while. I once overheard her telling a friend why it didn't work out between her and Dad. They were having coffee in the living room and I was reading in a tight space between the couch and the wall. They must not have known I was there because she started talking about how they married too young, and that Dad is an extrovert and she's an introvert. I guess that means my mom is on the shy side and my dad is more outgoing. I never asked though. I didn't want her to get mad that I heard.

"Love is strange," Mom says. "You don't really pick who you fall in love with. It picks you. And I'm excited for Daddy. As I said the other night, he deserves happiness."

"Do you think Ruby's mom is an extrovert?"

Mom gives me a funny look. "I don't know Sandhya very

well, only through you and Ruby. She seems friendly, if that's what you're asking."

"I just don't want anything to change," I say. "I want everything to stay the same. I like things the way they are."

"I know," my mom says. "Daddy and I both know that change is hard for you. That's one of the reasons he waited so long to tell you. We all hope that you and Ruby get closer because of this, and that Benji and Ruby will bond as well. We think it'll turn out to be a good thing for all of you."

I start crying. My mom sets down her juice and leans toward me, wrapping me in a hug. The problem is, her arms are squeezing me too tight and her fingernails are scratching my collarbone and my hair feels tangled and fuzzy against her shoulder.

"Why didn't I get straight hair like you and Benji?" I ask, pushing away from her. "Why did I have to get Dad's curls? They're driving me crazy."

"I'll get the detangler spray." Mom stands up. "I'll get a brush too. Want me to do braids?"

"Two," I say, wiping my nose with the back of my hand. "French braids."

My mom slides open the glass door and disappears into the kitchen. I sip the passion fruit juice and try to get back into my book, but I can't concentrate on a single sentence.

On the drive back to the city, Mom and Bill talk quietly in the front seat. My stepdad teaches chemistry at the same college where Mom works, so mostly they chat about their students and the other professors and who is working on what book for which university press. It's pretty boring.

Usually on the drive home, Benji and I play I Spy or we try to find as many states as possible on license plates, but this evening he conks out as soon as my mom buckles him in. It's better than puking and it's definitely better than him belting out love chants. Mostly I look out the window. It's staying light later now, which means summer is coming. That means I'm getting close to getting my dog. Mom and Bill have said I can bring her back and forth with me from the city to their house in Tomsville every weekend. Wow. In two short months I'll have a furry little Waffle or Maple sitting on my lap.

"I have to pee!" Benji shrieks.

We're just pulling into Manhattan. He's awake now, rubbing his eyes and bouncing around in his seat.

"We're almost there," Mom says. Then she turns to my stepdad. "Can you text Greg and ask him to come down?"

"Sure thing," Bill says.

As she double-parks in front of our building, Dad is already outside. I grab my backpack and jump out of the car, quickly followed by Benji, who is clutching his gut and doubling over in pain.

"Hey, guys," Dad says, wrapping us both in a hug. "Hey, Ellen. Hi, Bill."

Mom and Dad and Bill all greet one another with hand-shakes and cheek kisses. It's like this every Sunday night. If Mom can find parking they often come upstairs for coffee. Benji and I joke about how grown-ups will do anything for coffee.

"I really have to pee!" Benji says. "My bladder feels like Niagara Falls and Victoria Falls and have you ever heard of Inga Falls? That's in the Democratic Republic of the Congo."

I have no idea how my brother finds ways to incorporate geography into a bathroom emergency. Also I'm trying not to think about how he sounds like Ruby shrieking about having to pee all the time. It's not that I'm mad at Ruby. I just want to pretend that she and her mom don't exist right now.

"Can you please take Benji upstairs?" Dad says to me. "I want to talk to Mom and Bill for a minute."

"About what?" I ask. If it's about me I want to be around to hear it.

"I seriously have to pee," Benji pleads.

"Is it about me?" I ask.

"No," Dad says. "It's not about you."

"Willa," Mom says. "Listen to Dad and take Benji upstairs." She leans down and gives us both a kiss. "Love you guys. Talk tomorrow."

Benji mad dashes into our lobby, but I take my time crossing the sidewalk. I can see my dad stepping closer to my mom and gesturing with both hands.

Actually it would be good if they were talking about me, like *Willa refused to let me trim her toenails* or *Willa couldn't settle her body.* That's normal. That's what always happens. But if the conversation isn't about me, then it's probably about my dad and Ruby's mom. And judging by the way my mom is smiling and my stepdad is clapping my dad on the back, I'm guessing there's news. And I'm guessing it isn't good.

CHAPTER 7

When I get upstairs, there's a mini-trampoline in the middle of the living room. It's got royal-blue padding around the edges and a black mesh center. It's the exact trampoline we've been looking at online. The thing is, I've only gotten twenty-seven stickers on my chart. I've earned them for things like controlling my energy level or remembering my lunch and keys when we leave for school or not losing my water bottle on a weekly basis. My dad and I had a deal that I needed forty stickers before he would order the trampoline.

I flop facedown on the couch and donkey kick my feet behind me. I can hear the toilet flushing and the faucet running, and then Benji comes out of the bathroom rubbing his hands on his shorts.

"Cool!" he says, jumping onto the trampoline. "I thought you had to fill up that chart though."

"Exactly." I snap a bracelet against my wrist. Maureen lets me pick out a prize at the end of every session, and recently I've been getting rubber bracelets. "Dad is totally guilty of something."

Just then, Dad unlocks the apartment door. He scoops up both of our backpacks from the foyer and carries them into the living room.

"You found the trampoline," he says, smiling. "I figured you guys would be jumping. Don't forget to unpack your backpacks and put in your school stuff for tomorrow."

"Of course we found the trampoline," I say, rolling onto the floor and bicycling my feet in the air. "It's not like you hid it."

"Willa says you're guilty of something," Benji says. He's doing jumping jacks on the trampoline, his brown hair flying up like a minifigure's hair that has come detached from its head.

A funny look flickers across my dad's face. I consider refusing to touch the trampoline until I can get to the bottom of this. Except Benji is making the trampoline look like the best jumping experience ever and I can't resist much longer.

"Benji, time for your bath," Dad says. "It's Sunday night so I need to wash your hair and trim your nails."

Benji stops jumping. "What about dessert?"

"You can have dessert after your bath," Dad says. "Willa, come have dessert while Benji's in the tub. Then you can trade."

"But Mom braided my hair," I say as my brother skips into the bathroom. "I don't want to get it wet. I want to wear it like this tomorrow. And please no nails. Or at least just fingers. Please no toes."

"Meet me in the kitchen after you've unpacked," Dad says, tossing me my backpack. "You can take your bath without getting your braids wet. And I'll check your nails to see if we can put it off a few days."

Before I can protest, Dad goes into the bathroom to start Benji's bath. I realize that most eleven-year-olds have graduated to showers, but I can't stand them. Too many prickles poking my skin, too much water in my eyes. I'm not crazy about getting wet in the bath, either, but there's no way Dad would let me skip hygiene altogether. One time, after a big anti-bath protest, he said, "You don't want to be the kid at school with the stinky armpits." When I suggested I prevent stinky armpits by wearing deodorant like Norie and Zoe, who've been using it since fourth grade, Dad rolled his eyes and said, "Just . . . bath . . . now."

Once I'm in my room I put my dirty clothes in a pile for the hamper, and then I shake my clean clothes into a drawer. That's the deal that Dad and I have. As long as my clean things aren't dumped onto the floor, I can organize my clothes however I want. At Mom's house, she makes me fold my shirts and match my socks in pairs and put my underwear in the top drawer, my jeans in the bottom drawer.

"I don't get it," I say to Dad a few minutes later. I'm at the kitchen table eating apple slices sprinkled with cinnamon.

"Get what?" Dad asks, leaning against the counter. He's drinking seltzer with a slice of lime in it.

"Why did you get me the trampoline before I finished my chart? I had thirteen stickers left to go."

"Hang on." Dad calls for Benji to turn off the water in the tub. Benji shouts something back and then Dad says to me, "I figured you could use the sensory input. I definitely would have given you a sticker for the way you unpacked your backpack without a lot of reminders."

Sensory input is a big thing Maureen talks about. It means that my body needs pounding and squeezing and swinging and hard pressure in order to feel calm like a regular person's body.

"Benji can also use it for his parkour," Dad adds. "You can share the trampoline."

"So what about my chart?" I ask. "Do we just throw it away? Or do I start trying for something new?"

"I haven't really thought about that," Dad says. "I guess we'll consider that chart filled up. We can start the next chart soon. I'll email Maureen and ask her what she suggests."

Dad goes over to the sink and starts rinsing out our water bottles and filling them for school tomorrow. My water bottle is green and Benji's is red. My brother has the same water bottle he's had all year. When I started the school year I had a purple one, but I lost it by the end of September. Then I had a striped one, then one with little blue monsters on it. I've had this green once since early March, which is a record for me.

"Did you see Ruby this weekend?" I ask. "The other day at I Scream you asked if she wanted to play soccer."

Dad puts our water bottles in the fridge. I can tell he's stalling for time because he doesn't turn around for a while. Finally, he says, "We met this morning for bagels in the park and kicked around a soccer ball. Then it started to rain so we checked out Hex. You know that game-playing place on Broadway? Ruby plays a mean game of Exploding Kittens."

The apple suddenly feels sour and scratchy in my mouth. I spit the chewed-up bits into my hand and then hide them under the other apple slices. Dad hates when I spit out food but sometimes it's necessary, like if an avocado chunk is sliming up my salad, or if I just found out that my dad and Ruby played Exploding Kittens at a game store on Broadway.

"What were you talking about with Mom and Bill on the sidewalk?" I ask.

"Just some things," Dad says. Then he leans into the hallway and shouts, "Benji! I told you to turn off the water before you cause a flood!"

"It looked like you were telling them something and they were congratulating you," I say. "Was it about you and Ruby's mom?"

"I hadn't thought about that," Dad says.

"What?" I ask.

"About how it looked," he says vaguely. He's turning his phone around and around in his hand.

"You should start thinking about things more," I tell him.

There's a splash from the tub. Dad sets his phone on the counter and rushes toward the bathroom. On my way into my bedroom I jump on the trampoline a bunch of times, but it doesn't settle me down even a little bit.

....

On Monday morning, Ruby waves at me as she walks into the classroom. She's wearing her Manchester United soccer shirt and her hair is back in a ponytail.

"I like your French braids," she says.

"Thanks," I reply. I try not to think about how she played soccer and Exploding Kittens with my dad yesterday. I try to imagine that everything is normal, like it was last week at this time, two best friends with our single parents who we didn't know were secretly together.

It's hard to pretend that though. As Ruby fishes her water bottle out of her backpack, I watch her closely. I'm trying to figure out if she knows if something new is up, like what my dad told my mom and Bill on the sidewalk and why he bought me the trampoline several stickers early. Finally, as Ruby sits down next to me, I decide to probe a little.

"I heard you played soccer with my dad in the park," I whisper to her. No one else is around so it feels safe to talk about it for a second.

"Yeah—he's really good. It was fun. We went to Hex

too." Ruby giggles. "He was so funny about the different kittens on the cards. He had these hilarious names for—"

"Did they talk about anything else with you?" I ask, cutting her off. I definitely don't need to hear about his Dad Jokes. "Did you notice anything different between them?"

Ruby mashes her lips together, like she's surprised that I don't want to hear all about my dad's totally not funny jokes. Well . . . sorry. Sorry not sorry.

"Anything different how?" she asks, and her voice sounds a little frosty. "What are you talking about?"

"I don't know," I say, even though the truth is that I'm thinking about what Benji sang in the car, how first comes love, then comes marriage, then comes a baby in the baby carriage.

Ruby frowns. "Not really," she says after a long pause. "They seemed happy but they didn't kiss or anything."

"Shhhh!" I say. I quickly look around to make sure no one heard.

Ruby shakes her head. "Well, you asked."

"Not about that!"

I pick up my book and Ruby picks up her book and we stare down at our pages and don't talk to each other. I don't think we're in a fight but it's still kind of awful. Before last week, Ruby and I had never even had a second of tension between us.

A few minutes later, Ms. Lacey rings the bell to start the day. There's a tissue in her hand and she keeps wiping her nose. First we have morning meeting, and then we have math, where we are doing decimals and fractions to get ready for middle school. At ten fifteen, we shift to science. We're halfway through a lesson on alternative energy sources when Elijah, one of the LEGO-trading boys, raises his hand.

"Do you know when the middle school letters are coming?" he asks.

Ms. Lacey sighs. This happens at least three times a week now.

"Can this wait?" she asks. "Let's finish talking about solar power."

Elijah picks at a hole in the knee of his jeans. "I really want to get into Maya A. like my brother."

"I want to get into Cruz Hall," says another kid.

"You'll all get in somewhere," Ms. Lacey says, sneezing twice. Then she turns away to blow her nose. When she turns back, Avery has her hand high in the air, her fingertips pointing upward like the star on the top of a Christmas tree.

"Yes?" Ms. Lacey asks.

"My mom says this is the worst allergy season in years," Avery offers. "All the immunologists are saying it."

"I would definitely agree," Ms. Lacey says wearily. She looks tired and there are bluish-purple circles under her eyes.

"She could probably get you some free samples," Avery says. "Pharmaceutical companies are giving her eye drops and nose sprays all the time."

Ruby glances my way and rolls her eyes like *there goes Avery bragging again*. I have to slap my hand over my mouth to keep from laughing. It's partially about Avery but also I'm relieved that Ruby doesn't seem mad at me.

"Thanks, Avery," says Ms. Lacey, "but let's move on from allergies to solar power."

This other girl, Haley, raises her hand. "I heard the middle school letters are getting mailed out this week and I really want it to be Maya A. That's my top choice."

With that, it's like vinegar poured over baking soda. Instant chaos. Kids are shouting out Cruz Hall and Maya A. and The Tech School and Upper West Secondary. Avery is saying how she's auditioned for a performing arts school and she thinks she's going to get in. Some kids are moaning into their hands. The twins ask permission to get out their phones and text their mom. Finally, Ms. Lacey taps a ruler on a table to quiet everyone down.

"I realize this is scary and exciting," she says. "I'm not sure where you heard the news about the middle school letters, Haley. The latest we've heard from the Department of Education is that the letters are being mailed out next week, so—"

Everyone erupts again. I squeeze my hands on the edges of my chair. Maybe that's what my dad was talking to my mom about? No, he would have told me if it had to do with middle school. I slip off one of my bracelets and weave it around my fingers in a figure eight. One table away, Avery is fiddling with her charm bracelet, clanking the dogs nervously together. She doesn't look quite so braggy anymore.

Ms. Lacey never does finish the solar-power lesson. After calming us down about middle school, she tells us it's time to line up for gym. I'm walking down the hall, dreading whatever competitive sport the gym teacher is going to make us play, when Ms. Lacey touches my shoulder.

"Remember?" she asks.

I have no idea what she's talking about. I reach down and stretch out the cuffs of my leggings.

"Remember you're going to the guidance counselor during gym?" Ms. Lacey says. "You're meeting that girl."

"Oh, yeah." The outcast kindergartner. I forgot about that. I wish I'd worn shorts today. I thought these leggings were comfortable when I put them on in the morning but now they're pinching my ankles and squeezing behind my knees.

"If it works out, Mr. Torres will be expecting you in his office every Monday during gym."

The class has gone quiet and people are staring at me. I feel like a minifigure that's been separated from its legs. This is so embarrassing—*much, much* worse than the Think Chair. People get sent to the guidance counselor, Mr. Torres, for Big Problems, like if they're getting bullied or they have a rocky home life.

"Willa is going to be a peer mentor," Ms. Lacey tells the class. "There's a kindergartner who needs her help."

"No fair!" Avery calls out. "Why didn't we all get asked to be peer mentors?"

I think about what my mom said, about how Avery is jealous of me. When she said that, I totally didn't agree with her. Avery has made it clear since preschool that she thinks her life is better than mine. But as we pause in the hallway I notice her glaring at me, an envious look on her face.

Well, good. Let her be jealous.

I push through the doors, walk down two flights of stairs, and knock on the guidance counselor's door.

....

Back when I was in second grade and my parents were getting divorced, I spent a lot of time with the guidance counselor, playing board games or sometimes just crumpling paper into wads to get the fidgety feeling out of my hands. Mr. Torres is basketball-player tall with glasses and a shiny bald head. Now I only see him every few weeks in the halls. He always waves and high-fives me. I high-five him as quickly as possible. It's not like I want people to think I'm a frequent visitor to his office.

Mr. Torres greets me at the door, holds up his hand for a high five, and tells me I've gotten tall. The thing is, that's what every adult says to every kid they haven't seen in a while, as if they're expecting them to stay three feet forever.

There's a small girl sitting at the table in his office, a huge bin of LEGOs open in front of her. She has braids in the front of her hair that twist into three pigtails, and she's wearing a pink dress and striped leggings. She doesn't look like an outcast. She looks like a regular kindergartner, maybe a little on the small side.

Mr. Torres gestures in her direction and says, "Willa, this is Sophie. Sophie, here's Willa. She's the fifth grader I was telling you about."

"Hey," I say to Sophie, smiling over at her.

Sophie squints at me and then looks back down at the little blue car she's building. It has wheels and also wings and a bunch of lights on top.

As I sit down at the table across from her, Mr. Torres runs his hands over his smooth head and says, "I'll work at my desk while you two play."

"*Build*," I say out of habit. "Not play."

Anyone who loves LEGOs knows the difference. If you're acting out a story, you're *playing*. But if you're making something from scratch, it's building.

I glance around the office. The same posters are still on the walls from back when I was in second grade, like the one that says ROCK ON! with a picture of stones piled haphazardly on top of one another and lots of posters of puppies and kittens with cute captions. *Kittens*. *Exploding Kittens*—I really don't want to think about Ruby and my dad playing games yesterday so I quickly push that thought away.

"What do you want to build?" I ask Sophie.

She shrugs.

"You're making a car-plane?" I ask.

She shrugs again.

"I have a Race Car Driver minifigure that I never use," I say. "I'll bring it in next time and you can have it. I'm really into LEGO dogs. I'm building a dog kingdom at home. I've connected three baseplates, so it's going to be huge."

She doesn't look up, so I grab some green bricks and start building a car-plane too. I add gliders next to my wheels so it can take off from water as well as land. I think I'm supposed to be talking to her, so I ask her a few questions like who her teacher is and where she lives, but she never responds. After a while she starts humming a song from *Moana*. I hum along with her even though if anyone in my class heard me humming "How Far I'll Go" I'd be laughed out of fifth grade.

"Okay, girls!" Mr. Torres says brightly. He's standing above us and clapping his hands together.

Sophie and I both jump, startled. I was so busy building that I sort of forgot where I was. I think Sophie did too. I love that about LEGOs. They suck you in in the best possible way.

"It's time for me to bring Sophie back to her classroom," Mr. Torres says. "Willa, you can go up to the fifth floor on your own. This seemed to work out well. Same time next week?"

"Sure," I say.

We follow Mr. Torres into the hallway. We're about to say good-bye when Sophie holds up her fist and says, "Rock on, fifth grader."

Her voice is husky, lower than I expected, and she's missing one of her top teeth, so she looks like a jack-o'-lantern. Also, *rock on*? Like the poster?

"Rock on," I say, fist-bumping her back.

Maybe it's dorky but it's not like anyone is around to hear me. I watch her pigtails swing as she walks down the hall, and then I take the stairs two flights up and wait for my class to return from gym.

CHAPTER 8

I have a special way of walking to Maureen's
office so that no one from school knows where I'm going. I
head over to Columbus Avenue, slip into the pharmacy that
has stuffed giraffes and Playmobil sets in the window, and
browse the LEGOs in their small toy section. Sometimes
I buy a pack of gum if I have money, or I read the insides of
the greeting cards on the rack next to the school supplies.
I love cards with puppies on the front. After a few minutes I
can see through the front window that the crowd of people
leaving school has thinned out, so I cross over Columbus and
walk up to Ninety-Fifth Street.

Back when a sitter took me to Maureen's, we'd grab a
bagel or I'd eat a cereal bar on the way to my appointment.
Tons of kids leave school with nannies or parents and go to
lessons and classes. It doesn't look suspicious. But as soon as
I started walking alone, kids were like, *Where are you going?*
Want to go to Dunkin' Donuts? Can you come to the park?

Which is why I just say I have a math tutor. There's no way I'm telling people I go to an occupational therapist.

I ring Maureen's bell and wait for her to answer.

"Hi, Willa," she says, standing in the doorway of the gym and beckoning me inside. She pushes some hair off her face and adjusts her ponytail. Today she's wearing a blue T-shirt that says THIS ABILITY NOT DISABILITY on the front. "You know the routine."

Knowing the routine is a big thing for Maureen. And yet, as I walk into the gym today, I start hopping from side to side like popcorn pinging in a scalding pan. In my head, I'm hearing the routine—*untie sneakers, backpack in the corner, take out my water bottle, help set up our first activity.* But even though I know I should be doing those steps, I can't because I've just realized that I haven't seen Maureen since I found out about my dad and Ruby's mom.

I kick a purple yoga ball across the gym, then lean over and press the top of my head into a mat. It's not like I planned to do it. My body is moving without my mind telling it where to go.

"Your mom called this morning," Maureen says. She doesn't mention that I'm still wearing my sneakers and I'm currently upside down with my head pressed into a mat. "She said you were having a tough time settling your body this weekend."

I belly flop onto another yoga ball. As my backpack slides up and knocks my head, Maureen reaches into a drawer and hands me a weighted vest. I love weighted vests. They remind me of those heavy shawls they drape over you at the dentist when they're taking X-rays. I love those too.

"Your mom told me about your dad," Maureen says, sipping from her water bottle. "And your friend Ruby's mom."

I toss my backpack into the corner, slip the weighted vest over my head, and pry off my sneakers, one heel at a time. Usually Maureen wants me to untie my sneakers, but today she doesn't correct me. She knows when to push and when to let me be. Also, I like that Maureen talks to me like I'm a real person, not a kid. While I stretch and swing and roll on yoga balls, we always talk about our lives. I know that she's divorced and has a daughter and two grandsons. She's told me that she went into working with kids because she struggled growing up. She says that now people would call it ADHD, but back then she was just in trouble all the time.

"Want to swing?" Maureen asks. "It looks like you could use it. Why don't we set up the dachshund-dog swing?"

I smile gratefully. The vest is helping me feel more settled in my body. I don't even know the real name for the swing. It's a hot dog–shaped cushion that you sit on, and you pull yourself forward and backward. I once told Maureen that the swing looks like a dachshund, and the name stuck. She says she even calls it that with her other kids.

I find the dachshund-dog swing stored on a mat in the corner of the gym. It's heavy, so I have to wrap both my arms tight around it to carry it to the center. Maureen helps me hook it to the ceiling with ropes and thick metal clasps. I hop on, squeeze my knees in, and thrust my body back and forth. Once I've been going for a few minutes, a quiet calm washes over me. It reminds me of drinking lemon mixed with hot water and honey when I have a sore throat.

I started working with Maureen the winter that I turned five. I'd been seeing a different OT at a gym that had a clanky elevator and a chilly draft. That Christmas, we had a holiday performance at my preschool, and according to my mom, I got so overwhelmed by all the parents watching us that I took off my sneaker and threw it into the audience. If that wasn't drama enough, I also tried to hang from the twinkling string of lights, ripping them down. After that, my mom decided it was time to switch occupational therapists. She got me in to see Maureen, and I've been working with her twice a week ever since.

"I'm guessing the news from your dad upset you," Maureen says as I zoom past her on the swing. "It seems like it threw you out of sync."

I nod, remembering how my parents had a book when I was younger called *Your Out of Sync Child*. My mom stuck Post-its all over it. One morning they got in an argument about that book. That was back when they were fighting a lot. I remember wriggling under couch cushions and making Benji jump on me. Then they got mad about that and sent us both to our bedroom.

"I can't believe my dad is in love with Ruby's mom." I glance across the gym at Maureen's mini-trampoline. It's just like the one in our apartment. "Also, I think something else is going on and no one's telling me. Did you know that my dad gave me the trampoline last night? I still had thirteen stickers to go on my chart."

"That's nice you got your trampoline!" Maureen says. "I know you really wanted it."

I lunge my body forward but don't say anything. Yes, I wanted it. But I also want the truth about why I got it thirteen stickers early.

"I'm sure your parents have told you that change is inevitable," Maureen adds. "It's going to happen whether you want it or not."

I pull harder at the rope. Everyone says that about change but that doesn't make it easier to handle.

"I'm sure it still makes you feel awful," Maureen quickly adds. "All jumbled up and mad and maybe even wild inside."

Exactly, I think, but I don't have to say it out loud. Maureen gets me that way.

I finish on the dachshund dog, return it to the corner, and help Maureen hook up another swing. This one is an upside-down lollipop cushion. I sit on it and Maureen winds me tight and then lets go, sending me spinning in circles. She always makes me promise to let her know if I'm getting dizzy but so far that hasn't happened.

On my second time unwinding, I'm holding tight to the swing, whizzing so fast that the colors of the gym are blurry, like a rainbow pinwheel spinning into gray.

"You know, Willa," Maureen says, "sometimes you feel terrible and there's nothing to do but accept that it's happening and let yourself be in it."

At first I think she means the blurry spinning, but then I realize she's talking about the stuff with my dad and Ruby's mom.

"I guess," I say quietly.

At the end of our session, as I dig through the treasure bin for a stretchy bracelet, I don't feel as lousy as before. Somehow having permission to feel bad makes me feel a little bit better.

....

Maureen gives me a stick of wintergreen gum and I chew it for the whole walk home. When I get into the apartment, I'm surprised to discover Benji and our sitter, Joshua, on the couch playing Minecraft. Totally not fair! We're not allowed to have screen time on weeknights unless Dad is out for the evening. And if Dad is out for the evening, he always tells us the plan in the morning. This morning he just told us to pack our backpacks and hurry to the elevator.

I kick off my sneakers, drop my backpack on the floor, and flop onto the couch next to Benji.

"How many minutes have you had?" I ask. "And why are you getting Minecraft today? It's not a weekend."

Joshua is sitting on my brother's other side. I can see that they are working on Machu Picchu. Benji has been building it for a few weekends now. I usually build animal rescue centers but sometimes I help with Benji's temple. It took me two days to build a hundred stairs—and that's only on one side!

"He's had twenty-five minutes." Joshua glances at his phone on the coffee table. "I have the timer set. He has five more minutes."

I nod. I'm glad Joshua isn't letting Benji have unlimited screen time. Usually with Minecraft, we get thirty minutes each on Friday, Saturday, and Sunday. My parents talked about it and that's what they decided on. It's not a lot—like I know a ton of kids whose parents don't even know what games they're playing. But it's better than nothing.

"Can I go next?" I ask, watching as Benji puts walls around a secret chamber inside the temple.

"Definitely," Joshua says, touching his goatee. "Did you wash your hands yet? And unpack your backpack?"

I shake my head. On the bulletin board inside the front door my dad has made a checklist for my afternoon routine. I don't look at it much anymore. Usually I remember most things on my own.

"Do everything on your checklist," Joshua says, "and then you can have your turn."

"Why are we getting Minecraft?" I push off the couch and

hop onto the trampoline. I jump with both legs together and then one leg at a time. "Where's my dad going tonight?"

Joshua shrugs. "Don't know. He texted me a few hours ago and asked if I could stay late."

"Is he having dinner with someone?" I ask. Of course I'm thinking about Ruby's mom, but I don't say that because I don't know if Joshua knows they're together and I don't feel like being the one to tell him.

"I'm not sure," Joshua says.

I glance at Benji, wondering if he's going to blurt it out or do more of the kissing song, but Benji is fixated on the screen, sucking every bit of Minecraft out of his final few seconds.

Joshua glances at his phone again. "Willa, go ahead and do your checklist now."

He's using his warning tone. It's the same tone that my mom and dad use when I'm not listening. It's the tone that leads to strikes, and three strikes lead to consequences. Sometimes I don't care about consequences, but I'm not in the mood to go down the strike road right now.

"Fine." I jump off the trampoline and stomp into the kitchen, pounding my heels into the ground.

It's not that I'm mad at Joshua. We've had him as our sitter for two years, and Benji and I both like him. It's just that my dad always tells me ahead of time when he'll be out late, and now he's pulled a change on me without any warning.

I tug my lunch box and books out of my backpack and then dig around for my water bottle, but it's missing. Great.

Just great. Now I'll have to ask my dad to order another one, and he'll sigh like he's disappointed. Well, fine. Let him be. I'll tell him I'm disappointed right back.

The next night, Dad comes home in time for Taco Tuesday. But after he's done with the dishes, he closes himself in his bedroom for almost an hour. I can hear him talking on the phone in there. Dad often has work calls at night, but he always takes them on the couch with his laptop open on the coffee table. I usually lie on the couch reading with my feet in his lap, half listening to his boring conversations about building permits and zoning laws.

Tonight when Dad peeks into my room to tell me to brush my teeth, I ask, "Who were you on the phone with?"

"Sandhya," he says. Then he holds up a silver water bottle with the label still on. "I bought you a new bottle at Whole Foods today. I'll put your name sticker on it and fill it up for tomorrow."

"Thanks," I say.

"Can you try to keep track of this one until the end of the year?"

"It's not like I want to lose them. They just fall out of my backpack." I run my hands over the LEGOs on my floor, pushing my palms into the sharp edges. "What were you and Ruby's mom talking about?"

"A lot of things," Dad says. "We'll talk more about it soon. Now it's time to brush your teeth. And we didn't trim your toenails last night."

I ignore the part about my toenails. "When will we talk about it?"

"Dad!" Benji calls from the living room. "Can I read you this thing about the Archbishop of Canterbury? Did you know that he was killed by followers of the king in 1170 but the king didn't actually want him dead? It was an accidental assassination!"

"We'll talk about it all soon," Dad says to me.

"When?" I ask. This is getting really annoying.

"Dad!" Benji calls across the apartment. "Did you hear what I said about the Archbishop of—"

"Yes, I heard and I'm coming!" Dad calls back, laughing. Before he leaves he says to me, "Waggy, it's going to be okay. I promise."

As I stomp into the bathroom, I think about how Dad is hardly one to be making promises right now. And why does Benji care so much about the Archbishop of Canterbury's death from almost a thousand years ago when our life is falling apart right here in the present? I spit into the sink, watching the foamy toothpaste swirl in circles and disappear down the drain.

"We need to talk," I hiss-whisper to Ruby during quiet reading the next morning. "Can you get a bathroom pass? I'll get one first, and you wait a little bit and then meet me there."

"Okay." She glances quickly at Ms. Lacey, who is busy conferencing with Elijah and Haley. Elijah is sucking at his knuckles. No doubt they're talking about middle school letters. The tension in the air is so thick that no one can say the words *middle school* without someone starting to whimper. I can't believe that a week ago that was my biggest worry!

I grab a pass and hurry to the bathroom. A few seconds later, Ruby comes in. She glances behind her, making sure she didn't get followed. Ruby never gets in trouble at school, so she's nervous about breaking the rules. I'm more used to it from back when I couldn't control my body in school and frequently talked without raising my hand.

"What's up?" Ruby whispers. "You know we're not supposed to do meet-ups in the bathroom. Also I sort of have to pee, so we shouldn't talk long."

"I think something weird is going on," I tell her. "Was your mom out on Monday night?"

Ruby nods. "Yeah, I had a sitter."

"Me too . . . and they were on the phone forever last night."

"I guess so. My mom was in her bedroom and said she needed privacy."

"Exactly." I cross my arms over my chest. "Same with my dad."

Ruby flips the bathroom pass over in her hands. "So what's the problem? They were talking on the phone. Boyfriends and girlfriends do that. No big deal."

I hook two fingers around the collar of my shirt and pull hard, stretching it outward. "I think something else is going on with them," I say, deliberately ignoring the *boyfriend and girlfriend* part, "and I don't think it's good."

Ruby shakes her head. "Nothing *else* is going on. And you have to stop thinking this is so bad. My mom and Greg are cute together. You should have seen them last weekend. My mom was saying that maybe this Friday night we could all go to—"

"Stop!" I say, holding up my palm like a crossing guard. "I don't want to *all* do anything on Friday night! And he's not Greg, Ruby. He's not a *boyfriend*. He's *my dad*! Also, have you ever thought about what would happen if they broke up? What would that do to our friendship? Or, worse, what if they don't ever break up? Honestly, I think something else *is* going on and I'm going to get to the bottom of it."

Ruby shifts her weight from one foot to the other and then back again. I wonder if she finally gets what I've been trying to say since last week, that this is all bad, all terrible, no two ways about it.

But instead of agreeing, Ruby sniffs briskly and says, "I think you're being paranoid. Also, I actually have to pee. I should do that and then go back to the classroom."

"Paranoid?" I shoot back, letting go of my shirt. It droops limply from my neck but at least it's not choking me anymore. "No, I'm not! Remember last week when we were walking to I Scream and I said something was going on and you were like, *No . . . everything is fine*? Look who was right!"

Ruby bites her bottom lip. "I didn't mean it that way."

"Well, it sounded like you did!"

Just then, a teacher's assistant pokes her head into the bathroom. "Girls? Everything okay?"

"Yes," Ruby and I say in unison.

"Well, it's time to settle down and get back to your classrooms," she says in a snippy voice. "You know there's no socializing in the bathrooms."

Ruby glares at me like *thanks a lot for getting us busted* and then stomps into a stall, locking the door with a loud click. I spin in a half circle and walk angrily back to class, dragging my fingers along the wall the whole way.

At lunch, Ruby and I sit near each other but we barely talk. She eats her almond butter sandwich, which I can smell from across the table, and she talks to Haley about soccer. I listen in on their conversation while also chatting with the Robbins twins. Norie and Zoe gossip about their crushes, like who has long eyelashes and who has a zigzag buzzed into his hair. Even as I'm nodding along with them, I keep glancing over at Ruby, but she's not looking at me. She doesn't even roll her eyes in my direction when Avery shows off her mood-changing nail polish to everyone at our table. Even though I sort of think it's cool, like a mood ring you can paint, I won't give Avery the satisfaction of admiring it.

Right after lunch, as we're being herded into the recess yard, I don't see Ruby anywhere.

"Where's Ruby?" I ask Haley. She's kicking a soccer ball hard against the wall.

"She left after lunch to go to the orthodontist."

"Oh, right," I say, like I already knew and just forgot.

As I half-heartedly join a game of gaga, smacking the ball but not hitting anyone's shins, all I can think about is that I don't want to be in a fight with Ruby. It feels like we are though. It feels like everything with her mom and my dad is pulling us apart whether we like it or not.

CHAPTER 9

That evening, Dad gets home from work early.
He's carrying two Whole Foods bags and a bottle of wine.
I'm at the kitchen table doing homework. Benji and Joshua
aren't home yet. I think they're in Central Park. Usually that's
where Joshua brings Benji on sunny days to climb rocks and
practice his ninja moves.

"What's going on?" I ask, eying the grocery bags and
the wine.

"Sandhya and Ruby are coming for dinner!" he says
excitedly.

I lean over the back of a chair, letting the wooden points
press hard into my armpits. "When?"

Dad sets the paper bags on the counter and unpacks
cheeses and olives and brown takeout cartons. "They're getting here around seven. Sandhya has to finish writing a brief
at work. We'll eat a little late but I can cut up some veggies
now if you're hungry."

"What about taco bowls?" I ask. That's what we always have on Wednesday nights. We put the leftovers from Taco Tuesday into a bowl, sprinkle them with grated cheese, and heat them in the microwave. I love Taco Bowl Wednesday almost as much as Taco Tuesday.

My dad sets a baguette on the counter. "We'll have taco bowls tomorrow. Did you know that Ruby is lactose intolerant? Sandhya says that dairy bothers her a bit too."

"Of course I know that," I say. "Ruby is my best friend." I push my fingertips hard into my palms, because even as the words are coming out of my mouth I wonder if they're still true. Since Ruby and I have never had a fight before, I'm not sure where we stand now.

Just then, the front door unlocks, and Benji and Joshua walk into the kitchen.

"What's going on?" Benji asks when he sees my dad. He's holding a stack of library books in his hands. I can see that the top book is *Who Was Frida Kahlo?* and underneath that there's a world atlas. "Why're you home already?"

"Ruby and her mom are coming for dinner," I explain flatly.

"Ooooohhhhh!" Benji makes a wet, smoochy sound into his palm.

Joshua looks at my dad and my dad nods his head. I wonder if that means that Joshua knows, or if he's just realizing that we know. I also wonder if Joshua's new goatee is scratchy. When I asked him that the other day, he shook his head and said it felt fine, but I don't believe it. I'm glad I'm not going to have to deal with a beard someday, because I think they would itch like crazy.

"That's wonderful about you and Sandhya," Joshua says to my dad.

Dad smiles and starts to say something, but I quickly push back my chair and hurry out of the kitchen, except I'm not paying attention, so I slam into the doorframe, knocking my shoulder.

"Ow!" I yelp.

"Willa!" Dad says, rushing over. "Are you okay?"

"No," I say as I continue on to my room. "Definitely not."

For the next half hour, I play *Old Yeller* on audio book and chew gum and build LEGOs. The *Old Yeller* audio book is my top choice for when I'm feeling down. I always stop before the ending. When I first got it I listened to the whole book and got so upset I was flinging myself all over my bed, and my mom had to lie on top of me to settle me down. After that I learned to pause *Old Yeller* before chapter fifteen.

I'm at the part where Travis and Old Yeller are hunting squirrels when Dad comes in to check on my shoulder. I tell him it still hurts even though it's mostly better. Whatever. Let him feel bad.

Before he leaves my bedroom I remind him to put away my unfinished sticker chart and my checklists. We always hide those before friends come over. I don't need people seeing that I use checklists to remember to brush my teeth and pack my water bottle. That's personal.

A little while later I hear the doorbell ring. I hear Ruby's mom and my dad saying hello and I hear Benji launching into some fact about Frida Kahlo's paintings. I listen hard but I can't hear Ruby's voice. I wonder if she's as annoyed as I am about this last-minute dinner party and decided to stay home with a sitter.

A minute later there's a knock on my door.

I pause *Old Yeller.* "Come in!"

"Hey," Ruby says, stepping into my room.

"You came," I say.

Ruby gives me a funny look. "Of course I came." Then she pushes aside some LEGOs and books and sits cross-legged on my floor. "Notice anything different about me?"

I spit my gum into a wrapper, crumple it in my palm, and study Ruby. She has on the same Adidas shirt and slippery soccer shorts that she was wearing at school this morning. But then she opens her mouth wide, tilts her head up, and says, "Aaaaaaaah!"

"You got your palate expander off!" I say, rolling onto my knees and looking into her mouth. I've only known Ruby with a mouthful of metal but it's all gone now. "Did it hurt?"

"Not really." Ruby snaps a few red bricks together and pulls them apart again. "It hurt going on but then I got used to it. Now it feels strange *not* to have a palate expander in.

I keep running my tongue over the top and bottom of my mouth looking for it."

I'm glad I don't have to get a palate expander because I'd probably tear it off my teeth on the first day. I don't even like tags or seams so I can't imagine metal poking my mouth. I'm hoping I don't need braces either. My dentist says it's too soon to be sure.

As I return to building, Ruby begins organizing my LEGOs into piles of greens, blues, yellows, and reds. That's so Ruby, to make things neat and tidy. I have to resist the urge to take my hands and swirl her ordered piles into a kaleidoscope of color. After a few minutes, I forget that she called me paranoid in the school bathroom this morning and I forget that I snapped at her and I forget that her mom and my dad could quite possibly be exchanging wet smooches in the kitchen at this very moment. When I forget all that it feels like we could just be hanging out like usual, nothing to do with our parents. Ruby lies back on my floor and holds her phone above her head. She often watches soccer clips or looks at videos that people are talking about at school. My parents won't let me click on a video without their permission, but Ruby's mom is more laid-back about that.

"Eeeewwww!" Ruby shouts.

I look up quickly. She has her flashlight on and she's peering under my bed.

"This is so gross!" she says. "You've got bunched-up socks under there and gum wrappers and dust bunnies and . . . is that underwear?"

"Stop it!" I snatch her phone out of her hand and turn the flashlight off. She has no right to look under my bed at the things I've cast off because they have bad seams or too-tight elastic.

Ruby laughs. "You should clean under there or you're going to start growing fungus and crud."

"I clean under there," I say, even though I totally don't. "I just haven't in a while."

"Sorry," Ruby says, shrugging. She reaches for her phone and slides it in the pocket of her shorts. "I was just joking. You don't have to get so mad."

I shrug and go back to building LEGOs.

"I *am* actually sorry," Ruby says. "I didn't mean that about fungus and crud."

"It's okay," I say. Because the truth is, the last thing I want is to be in a fight with my best friend. "I'm sorry about how I snapped at you in the bathroom this morning."

"It's okay back," Ruby says.

"Dinner's ready!" Ruby's mom shouts from the kitchen. "Willa! Ruby! Benji! Come to the table."

Ruby shrugs and heads out the door. I hear Benji scampering across the apartment. I press my hands into the floor, spreading out my fingers and pushing into the rough texture of the LEGOs.

"Willa?" Dad calls out. "Are you coming? We're ready to eat."

I stand up slowly, touch the nose of the golden retriever in my poster, and walk out to join them at the table.

....

It's not Taco Bowl Wednesday but I have to admit the food is good. Dad cut up chunks of cheddar with slices of baguette, which he knows I love, and he got pitless kalamata olives, which I also love. I won't eat anything with pits or seeds in it because I hate being surprised while I'm chewing. Everyone else is eating chicken but Dad got sesame-crusted tofu for me.

"When did you become a vegetarian, Willa?" Ruby's mom asks, dabbing her napkin against her lips.

"When I was five," I tell her. I pluck at a rubber band around my wrist, twisting it around my finger and then rolling it off.

"What made you become a vegetarian?" she asks. "I know your dad loves his steak and burgers. Is your mom a vegetarian too?"

I glance worriedly at Dad. Ruby's mom has met my mom at various classroom potlucks this year, and Ruby and I have always been excited to yank our moms into conversation. But now that Ruby's mom is with my dad—my mom's ex-husband—it makes me feel nervous to talk about my mom.

"Ellen eats chicken and fish," Dad says, sipping his wine. "Willa is the only vegetarian in the family."

"I just don't like meat," I say, which isn't the whole truth. I don't want to go into the details about how, when I was five, I looked at a hamburger and could picture the cow the moment it got slaughtered and how it must have fallen dead onto the ground. Once when I was younger I tried to explain this to my mom. She looked so horrified that I decided it's better just to tell people I don't like meat.

"Want to do best part worst part?" Ruby's mom asks everyone. "Ruby told me how you taught it to her, and we've even added a new part that we do—"

"No!" I shout. I don't mean to be so loud, but there's no way I can play my mom's and my game right now, with my dad and his new girlfriend. Maybe that sounds harsh but it's the truth.

Dad clears his throat. Ruby's mom quickly launches into a story about something that happened at work. Benji shares some fact about Frida Kahlo and her husband, another Mexican painter named Diego Rivera. Ruby quietly picks at her chicken.

When dinner is over, we're carrying our plates to the counter when Ruby's mom announces, "I have a treat for everyone. I brought ice cream and sorbet and a bag of gummy bears to celebrate Ruby getting her palate expander off."

"Yes!" Benji exclaims, pumping his fist in the air. "We never get sweet desserts on school nights!"

Dad ruffles my brother's hair. "Tonight we do."

I make a face at Dad. This is something he's really strict about—no sugar before bed. I don't like how he's suddenly acting like sweets at night are no big deal.

"Greg and Ruby and Benji," Ruby's mom says, "go out to the living room and wait for us. Willa and I will bring out dessert."

As they disappear into the living room, I lean against the counter, rolling my ankles inward. I can hear Benji doing ninja kicks on the trampoline and Dad asking Ruby about her soccer teams. Then he makes a crack about how Cinderella was dropped from the soccer team because she kept running away from the ball, and Ruby laughs like it's hilarious. I want to stomp in there and tell her: *Do NOT laugh at his Dad Jokes. Seriously. Don't encourage him.*

"Willa," Ruby's mom says, opening the door to the freezer, "want to get out the spoons?"

Now I can hear Ruby hopping onto the trampoline. Benji is telling her a riddle and Dad and Ruby are both laughing. Ruby was so quiet at dinner, but as soon as I'm gone it sounds like she's having a blast. My arms and legs are pulsing with energy. I suddenly want to squeal or knock something over.

Ruby's mom takes out the ice cream and sorbet and then reaches into the cupboard for the bowls. I don't like how she knows where our bowls are, but it's not like I can tell her that. I walk slowly to the silverware drawer, slide it open, and start counting *one, two, three*—

103

"I wanted to check in and see how you're doing with everything going on," Ruby's mom says. "I know you were upset that day at I Scream."

I squeeze the spoons tightly in my fist. "I'm fine."

"That's good. I know it's a lot to take in."

As I start counting spoons again, Ruby's mom sets her hand on my shoulder and says, "Also, please call me *Sandhya*. I'm not just *Ruby's mom* to you now."

I open my hand and the spoons crash with a loud clatter onto the floor.

"Everything okay in there?" Dad calls from the living room.

"Yes," Ruby's mom says. "Just fine."

I sink onto my knees and sweep together the spoons. I can hear Ruby and Benji jumping together on the trampoline now. If I were out there I'd crawl under the trampoline and let the center part press down on my back. Except I couldn't do that because it's weird and Ruby is here and I only do weird things like that in private. The problem is, my private world and the rest of the world are colliding, and there's no place I can be myself.

CHAPTER 10

For the whole weekend, all I can think about is Puppapalooza. It's a dog festival taking place this Sunday at Union Square. As soon as I saw a sign for it at a bus stop I told my parents that I absolutely *had* to go, so they switched around the days we're at Mom's. Mom and Bill drove us to Tomsville on Friday night and Dad is picking us up Sunday morning.

Knowing that Puppapalooza is happening, I'm amped all weekend. I can't stop wiggling at lunch on Saturday, and Mom has to keep reminding me to put my knees down. She tries to trim my toenails but I shriek and kick her away. That afternoon, when Benji is reading a book on flags that Bill bought for him, I get into his face with Woofers, my stuffed dog, and start barking. I thought it would be funny but Benji shouts for me to leave him alone. That's when Mom tells me to get my sneakers and sweatshirt because we're going for a walk.

Usually I like walking with my mom. We do a loop from her house, around a park, past a few shops, and back into her neighborhood. But the problem today is that all she wants to talk about is if I'm feeling better about my dad and Ruby's mom and whether it helped settle my body to see Maureen this week.

"I don't know," I keep saying.

The more she talks about it, the more I want to run away and roll around in nearby lawns. I settle for skipping and kicking my heels into my butt. We've been walking for about fifteen minutes when Mom pauses in front of a low brick building with a bunch of windows and a parking lot on the side. There's a sign near the street that says TOMSVILLE MIDDLE SCHOOL.

"It's a great school," she says. She pushes up her glasses on her nose and squints like she's thinking hard. "Our neighbors' kids go there. And get this—all you have to do is show up. No testing, no application process."

I glance at the building. I'm sure we've driven by it before but I've never really noticed.

"The Children's School sent an email to the parents saying that your middle school letters are going out this week," Mom says.

I nod. "Everyone at school is freaking out."

"Are you?"

"I wish I could stay at The Children's School," I say. "I wish they went up through eighth grade or even high school."

Mom takes off her glasses, rubs a smudge off the lenses, and puts them on again. "Willa, I know that change is hard

106

for you, and I'm sorry so much of it is happening at once. I want you to understand that I would only bring this up if I really thought it was important. Daddy and I have been talking about it, and we were thinking that coming here for middle school could be an option. That would give you some space from Daddy's new relationship. Also it could make sense because you have to change schools in the fall anyway."

It takes me a second to realize she's pointing at Tomsville Middle School.

"We were thinking you could move here from Monday through Friday," she says. "It would be the reverse of what you're doing now. You could live with Bill and me during the week, and go to school here, and then go to New York City on—"

"I don't call him Daddy anymore," I say quickly. "I haven't for a long time."

I push off with my feet and run ahead of her. I run until my lungs are cold and I'm doubled over panting. When Mom catches up with me she takes my hand and squeezes it. We don't talk about Dad or Ruby's mom or Tomsville Middle School for the rest of the walk.

....

When Dad arrives on Sunday morning to pick us up, I don't tell him what Mom said about me moving to Tomsville. If he knows anything about it, he doesn't let on, though I do notice him talking quietly to Mom as we're buckling into the back seat.

Dad hands us bagels to eat in the car on the way into the city. Benji wolfs down his sesame bagel with cream cheese, but I nibble around the edges of my cinnamon-raisin. I try not to breathe in the sour smell of cream cheese or think about how slimy it would feel slithering past my tongue. I honestly can't believe people choose to eat cream cheese. It's 100 percent gross to me.

As we get closer to Manhattan I wrap my bagel in tinfoil, hand it forward to Dad, and ask for his phone so I can read about Puppapalooza.

"Oh wow!" I say, scrolling down his screen.

"What is it?" Benji leans over to look but I cradle the phone in my hands. The last thing I need is for him to get carsick and puke up his bagel and then we have to miss Puppapalooza.

"It says there are six rescue places where we can sign up and even do preliminary interviews to make sure we're a good family. We should get a rescue dog, right? That would be so cute. There's a petting area with puppies who are looking for forever homes. There's a stage with bands like Howl at the Moon and Dog Daze. There are even dog-themed treats for people to eat."

"Dog-themed treats?" Dad asks, glancing in the rearview mirror.

"I'm not eating dog food," Benji says, wrinkling his nose. "Those are definitely not going to be vegetarian, Willa."

I shake my head. "No, it's people cookies in the shape of dog biscuits. And they're selling kettle corn and calling it kibbles."

"Maybe we can drink water from a dish!" Benji offers.

"Totally!" I say, laughing and pushing my body against my seat belt.

A text appears on Dad's screen.

Sandhya: We decided to join at Puppapalooza after all! We are getting off the subway at 14th Street.

I briefly consider deleting this text and pretending it never happened.

"Did a text just come in?" Dad asks from the front seat.

"Ruby's mom," I say. My voice suddenly feels hoarse. "She says they're getting off the train at Fourteenth. Are they coming to Puppapalooza? Why didn't you tell us?"

"Uhh . . . uhhhh," Dad says, stuttering a little. "She said there was a cold going around her office and she and Ruby were going to stay home and rest. They must have changed their minds."

"Ruby's coming?" Benji asks. "Does she even like dogs?"

"Who doesn't like dogs?" Dad says. "Willa, I would have told you if—"

"But this was MY plan," I say angrily. "You should have asked me if it was okay."

I don't add that I feel a little weird about being around Ruby's mom since she asked me to call her Sandhya last week and said that she's no longer just Ruby's mom to me now.

"Isn't Ruby your best friend?" Benji asks. "Why wouldn't you want her to come?"

"Can't you shut up for a second?"

"Willa!" Dad says. "We don't say *shut up* in this family."

"It's not like we *don't* say it," I grumble. "It's that you don't *want us* to say it but we still do."

"Good point," Benji says.

"Willa," Dad warns, and I can tell by his tone that he's about to start counting to three, and by three he'll threaten to take something away. I pick at the edge of my seat and stare out the window.

"I didn't say anything about it because I didn't think they were coming," Dad says. "And I thought you'd be happy to have Ruby come along. I'm sorry if I misread things."

I sigh heavily and hand the phone back to Dad. "Do they have to come? I just want this to be a family thing. And please don't start saying they are family now because they're not."

"Willa," Dad says. "I know you're upset but . . . yes. They're coming. It sounds like they're actually already here."

I yank off my socks and toss them onto the floor of the car. "Fine," I say, shrugging. "It's all great. Yay."

Dad's phone lights up with a bunch of texts and emojis. Dad is driving, so Benji leans over to look.

"Ruby is texting you," he says to Dad. "She's saying, *Tell Willa I'm excited to see her*, and then she has a lot of dogs and hearts and flowers and a soccer ball."

"Since when did Ruby get your number?" I grumble.

"Sandhya put it in her phone," Dad says. "Emergency contact."

"Do you want to write back?" Benji asks.

"Stop looking at Dad's phone or it'll make you puke," I say. I don't comment on the *emergency contact* part or the fact that Ruby is texting my dad. None of this is good. Not one little bit.

Even though Ruby's mom and my dad are holding hands and looking way too in love, it doesn't ruin Puppapalooza. As soon as we arrive, Ruby, Benji, and I dart from booth to booth collecting flyers on rescue shelters and doggy camps and grooming salons. We wait in line to go into trucks with cages of rescue dogs that need to be adopted. We get free poop bags and paw-shaped key chains, and we take turns sitting on a beanbag chair and reading to a chocolate Lab. But the best part is the puppy playpen. Ruby and I spend forever nuzzling the puppies and letting them nibble our arms with their sharp teeth. Before we leave, Ruby gets out her phone and takes a bunch of pictures of me with a tiny black puppy. If I had a phone I'd totally be taking a million dog pictures now too.

"I'll text them to your dad," Ruby says, tapping at her screen. "So you can have them."

"Uhh," I say, burying my face in the puppy's soft pink belly. Even though I really don't like the idea of her texting with my dad, I *would* like the pictures to look at later and even share with my mom.

Ruby looks up from her phone. "Are you mad or something?"

I shake my head. "No, it's all just weird."

"Good weird or bad weird?"

I shrug. I don't know how to answer that, so I scratch behind the puppy's ears and say, "Thanks for texting the photos. I'm totally in love with this dog."

"If you got that dog," Ruby says, scratching his ears with me, "it would definitely be Pepper."

"Or Midnight."

"Or Inky."

She grins at me and I grin at her and then we slip out of the puppy playpen and join our parents. Benji is already with them, hoisting himself onto nearby scaffolding and clinging tight with his hands, slowly pulling his chin up to meet the bar.

"Can we please get our dog now?" I ask Dad as my brother drops from the scaffolding, landing with a hard smack on his feet. We all begin to walk to the concession area. "We could adopt that little black puppy. And it's almost May. That's only two months early."

Dad shakes his head. "We have to wait until school is out. You need to be around for a puppy. It's not fair to leave it home alone all day."

I wiggle my bare toes. At first it felt good not to have socks on but now I'm feeling all the creases and bumps inside my sneakers.

Ruby, Benji, and I run over to the food trucks. Dad buys us three bags of kibbles and bottles of water. Ruby's mom and my dad get coffee, and we sit down at a table near the stage to listen to music and munch our popcorn.

After a while, Ruby rests her head on her mom's shoulder and rubs her eyes with the palms of her hands.

"Tired?" her mom asks.

Ruby coughs a little. "My head hurts. I don't feel well."

Her cheeks are pink and I can see that she's barely eaten anything.

Ruby's mom touches her forehead. "You feel hot, sweetie. Does your throat hurt?"

Dad leans over and presses his palm against Ruby's cheek. I look away quickly. I don't want to see him acting like he's Ruby's dad all of a sudden.

"You did say there's something going around your office," Dad says to Ruby's mom.

"I really don't feel well," Ruby says, coughing harder into her elbow. "I want to go home."

"Do you think there was butter in the kettle corn?"

Sandhya says. "It said it was dairy-free. Maybe I should give you a Lactaid pill."

"I barely even ate any," Ruby moans. "And it's not my stomach. I just feel . . . terrible."

"Why don't we drive you home?" Dad says. "Our car is parked around the corner."

I tug at a bracelet on my wrist. I don't want to be mean but there are *hours* left of Puppapalooza and dozens of dogs left to pet. I'm definitely not ready to leave.

Ruby's mom starts to say something but then catches my eye. "Thanks, Greg," she says quickly. "We're fine. We'll take a cab home."

"Are you sure?" he asks.

She murmurs something to him, and before I know it their lips are touching. I pull so hard at the rubber band on my wrist that it breaks and falls onto the pavement.

....

We end up staying at Puppapalooza until the end of the festival. The best part is that Dad has a conversation with a woman from a rescue place called Manhattan Mutts. She tells him that they're bringing up a batch of dogs from South Carolina in late June and that there should definitely be a puppy for us. They exchange phone numbers and promise to stay in touch. At around five, Benji and I skip to the side street where we parked the car, our arms full of freebies and flyers.

"I'm going to sleep with the dog in my bed," I say as Dad merges onto the West Side Highway.

"Me too!" Benji says.

"We could trade nights," I say. "That's only fair."

Dad clears his throat. "A lot is happening this summer."

"Like what?" I ask. "Other than a dog?"

"There's something I need to talk to you both about," Dad says. Then he clears his throat again. "You know, a car ride is a great place to have an honest conversation."

My legs start trembling. All I can think is: *This is it*. I *knew* something was going on when Dad got me the trampoline early, and I *knew* something was going on when he went out for dinner with Ruby's mom, and I definitely knew when he was shut in his room talking to her on the phone for hours. I wasn't being paranoid like Ruby said! I was being realistic.

"It's about Sandhya and me," Dad says.

"Dad!" I scream. I bounce up and down and kick hard at the back of my seat. I'm going from zero to sixty and I can't stop it. "Just tell us! Tell us! Tell us!"

And so he does.

Dad tells us that when Ruby and her mom moved to New York City from Connecticut last summer, they signed a two-year lease on their apartment. But Ruby's mom just found out that the landlords who own their apartment are breaking the lease, which means she has to move. She's been looking all over for a new apartment these past few weeks, but then Dad and Ruby's mom decided that since they were planning to get engaged in the fall, they may as well do it sooner and get married this summer, and then we'd all move in together.

"Isn't a lease a contract?" Benji asks. "Are those people allowed to break it?"

For a smart kid, Benji can be a dummy sometimes. Talk about missing the forest for the trees!

"You and Ruby's mom are getting *married*?" I lean as far forward as my seat belt will let me. "But that's not possible. You *just* told us you were together."

"I'll explain about the lease later, Benji," Dad says. "And yes, Sandhya and I are engaged. I gave her an engagement ring last night but we wanted to tell you kids first before she wears it."

"You got engaged last night?" I ask, my voice rising in horror. "Does Ruby know?"

"She's going to find out this evening as well. Sandhya and I agreed that we'd talk about it with our own children first," Dad says. "And it's something we've been talking about for a while . . . but we made it official last night."

"But you just told us . . . hang on . . ." I pause, counting back on my fingers. "You just told us you were together ten days ago. How can you be getting married all of a sudden?"

"I realize this *seems* like it happened quickly," Dad says, "but we've been together since last September and we're ready to take the next step."

"I still don't understand about the lease," Benji says.

Something hits me. "Hang on. Are we moving?"

Dad's phone rings. He mutes it with his finger. "We're staying in our apartment. It's big enough."

"So who gets what room?" I ask.

"I want to keep my room," Benji says.

"I was actually thinking that Willa and Ruby could take the big room," Dad says, "and Benji can move into the little room. Or Ruby can have the little room since she's never had siblings before, and you and Benji can go back to sharing the big room."

"But I love my room!" I shout. There's no way I'm giving up my Girl Cave with my LEGOS and my body sock and my mess that's all my own! Also, how can Ruby live with us *all the time*? She doesn't even know I have a body sock. She doesn't know that my dad wears my striped socks over his black work socks every morning to pre-stretch them for me. Because that's what it's like with friends. A friend is nice to have over, but friends *go home*. They don't stay forever.

"We'll figure it out," Dad says. "The room arrangements are up for discussion."

I glance over at Benji, hoping he'll tell my dad that he's too much of a geezer to get married. That's when I notice that my brother's face has a sickly green hue.

"Were you reading?" I ask, pointing to the dog pamphlets in his hand.

But instead of answering, Benji hunches over and heaves chunks of bagel and kettle corn all over his lap.

"Great," I say, plugging my nose and trying not to look. "Just great."

"It's okay." Dad flashes his blinkers and steers off the highway. He always keeps paper towels and bags and cleaning spray in the car in case Benji pukes.

"It's okay," Dad says again. "It'll be okay."

"No, it won't," I say, but no one seems to hear me.

CHAPTER 11

Ruby isn't at school on Monday and that's fine with me. I'm not mad at her but I'm definitely mad at the fact that her mom is marrying my dad. No, actually, I'm a little mad at Ruby too. If she weren't so excited about their relationship, then maybe our parents wouldn't have decided to *take the next step*. Like, Ruby and I could have banded together and opposed the boyfriend-girlfriend thing until they clearly saw it was a terrible idea and returned to being regular parents.

That's why I haven't called Ruby to check if she's sick or to talk over the big news. My dad told me that Ruby knows about the engagement, but I don't feel like hearing her say how much fun this is going to be and how we'll have family game nights and things like that. Plus, if Ruby wanted to talk badly enough, she could have called me, and so far I haven't heard from her.

In addition to being mad at the news in general, I also don't want to give up my Girl Cave and have to share a room with Benji or with Ruby. And I don't want Ruby and her mom to move in and bring their lavender-scented soaps into our apartment. I don't want new smells, new furniture, new foods in the fridge, like soy cheese and lactose-free milk. But mostly I don't want to hide who I am, all the Private Willa stuff, in my own home.

Oh, and did they even think about the fact that they could get married and it wouldn't work out and they'd fight all the time and get divorced? Then where would that leave all of us?

I'm not the only one in a bad mood. The whole class is grumpy because of the middle school letters. Kids are drumming their fingers and bending paper clips and fighting for bathroom passes. Norie and Zoe go to the nurse for stomachaches. They're nervous because they both want to go to The Tech School—their parents liked the curriculum and they liked all the cute boys they saw on the tour—and they're freaking out about what happens if one twin gets in and the other doesn't.

As we're headed to gym Avery whispers to me, "Don't you have that girl on Mondays?"

Oh, I'm mad at Avery too. I hate that she was right when—that morning after we found out our parents were dating—she told Ruby and me that my dad and Ruby's mom looked like they were headed toward marriage when she saw them at the Italian restaurant. If she finds out that her prediction is true, she'll definitely be rubbing it in.

"What girl?" I ask Avery now as we're pausing in the hallway while Ms. Lacey tries to get everyone to quiet down.

"You don't remember?" she asks, rolling her eyes like I'm stupid. "That kindergarten girl you go to therapy with!"

I stare at my feet, my cheeks burning. Why is it that I never have a comeback when Avery is around? Going to the guidance counselor isn't therapy! Not that there's anything wrong with the guidance counselor OR therapy, but Avery definitely makes it feel that way.

Ms. Lacey cranes her head down the line. "Everything okay? I really need everyone to be quiet or we'll never make it to gym."

"Everything is fine," Avery says, adjusting her silver headband. She's also wearing a silver-and-white tank top and silver shoes. "I was just reminding Willa that—"

"It's okay," I call out. "I'm just heading down to see that girl, Sophie."

"Of course," Ms. Lacey says. "Thanks for remembering."

Avery huffs. "It was actually me who—"

I push through the doors before Avery can gloat about her amazing memory on top of everything else amazing in her life.

When I arrive at Mr. Torres's office, he greets me with a cheery "Hello, Willa!" and directs me to the table where Sophie is building.

"Hey, Sophie," I say.

Sophie looks up at me but doesn't say anything. She's

wearing a green T-shirt with a picture of a minifigure on the front, and below that it says DO THE LEGOMOTION. From the looks of it, she's constructing another car-plane.

"Darn!" I say, sitting down. "I was going to bring you my Race Car Driver minifigure. I'm sorry I forgot. It's been a crazy week."

Sophie shrugs. If I hadn't heard her say *rock on* last week, I wouldn't believe she actually talks. I'm glad she's not talking, though, because I really don't want to go into the craziness of the past week and specifically what I found out yesterday afternoon.

As I'm sinking my hands into the LEGO bin, Sophie slides the cutest little LEGO poodle across the table to me. I eye it curiously. She pushes it even farther in my direction.

"For me?" I ask.

When she nods, her brown eyes open big and she smiles, revealing her toothless window.

I lean into her and quietly ask, "Where did you get it?"

She gestures to the pocket of her jeans.

"You brought it from home?"

Sophie nods again.

"Wow," I whisper. "Thank you. I'll add it to my dog kingdom."

I'm talking quietly so the guidance counselor doesn't hear us. Adults never understand LEGO trading, and they often want to bust it up to prevent hurt feelings and demands of no-trade-backs.

"I'll definitely bring the Race Car Driver next Monday," I say, tucking the poodle into my pocket. "I'm sorry I forgot."

For the rest of the period we build a prison together. Sophie doesn't talk so it's not like we plan it out loud. She just builds a wall and I add a window with bars and she adds another window with bars and we populate it with a bunch of minifigure prisoners and guards wielding swords. When Mr. Torres tells us it's time to clean up, Sophie grins mischievously and knocks over a wall. I smile back at her as I knock over the other walls, and then we both knead the structure until it's a heap of bricks.

As we're leaving, Sophie holds up her fist to bump me, just like last week. "Hang in there, fifth grader," she says.

I glance around the walls of Mr. Torres's office. Sure enough, there's a poster of a kitten hanging upside down from a limb with a caption that says, HANG IN THERE.

The kid is definitely weird. But I also sort of like her. I fist-bump her back and return to class.

....

At occupational therapy that afternoon, Maureen asks how I'm doing. I swivel around on the spinny stool at her desk as I tell her about Puppapalooza and how my dad told us he's marrying Ruby's mom and then Benji puked and I might have to give up my bedroom. I'm about to tell her how this is happening on top of middle school letters and my mom suggesting I move to Tomsville when Maureen places a stretchy band in my hands.

"Pull this," she says, taking my backpack off my shoulders and setting it by the door. "And I'm going to get you some gum. The good sugary stuff."

I pull the band between my hands and watch as Maureen digs through her desk and produces Hubba Bubba. It's the kind of bubble gum you get on Halloween and never see again for the rest of the year. "I keep this around for emergencies," she explains, handing me a piece. "The sugar-free gum is fine for most chewing needs, but when your mouth really needs to chomp there's nothing like a wad of Hubba Bubba."

I unwrap the gum and grind my teeth in, letting the sugary juice seep around my tongue.

Maureen hooks the dachshund-dog swing to the ceiling. "We're going to get you swinging as you keep on telling me what's bothering you."

I stoop over to untie my sneakers. I'm already starting to feel better. It's good to be here.

"Okay," Maureen says as I climb onto the dachshund-dog swing and she hands me the rope to pull myself. "What part is feeling worse: your dad getting married or that it's your best friend's mom?"

I flatten the gum against the roof of my mouth with my tongue. "I don't know. I really want to just stay friends with Ruby. I don't want her to move in. I don't know why she's so excited about it. Also, it's all happening so fast."

"Maybe they're ripping off the Band-Aid," Maureen says. "Doing it quickly so you guys can start dealing with it."

"But I hate ripping off Band-Aids!"

Maureen says that's how it is for most sensory kids. I hate ripping off Band-Aids almost as much as I hate getting my toenails trimmed. Whenever I have a Band-Aid on, I get nervous about how much it's going to sting when it comes off. Ripping isn't even an option. First my dad tries for a slow peel but that gets me screaming. Then he tries to soak the Band-Aid with a washcloth. That sometimes works. Usually he leaves it on until it's shriveled and black around the edges and it eventually falls off in the bath.

"Let's get your belly on this," Maureen says as she gestures me onto a yoga ball, "and tell me what else is bothering you."

As she rolls me around on the ball, I tell her how I don't want to give up my Girl Cave and I don't want to share a room with Ruby and how she said I was growing fungus and crud under my bed because I had socks and gum wrappers down there. When we're done I flop limply onto the mat, spit my gum into a tissue, and reach for my water bottle. Maureen takes this downtime to brush my arms and legs with a soft plastic brush. She often does this at the end of a session.

"I also don't like the idea of their soaps in our apartment," I say, resting my head on the mat. "They have a lot of them. I mean, it's fine at their apartment but it would change the smell of our apartment. I like how our apartment smells."

"A lot of sensory people don't like perfumed things," Maureen says. "I'm guessing you'll never wear perfume when you're older."

"Definitely not," I say, shaking my head. Perfume seems disgusting. Just like how I can't imagine wearing makeup. Makeup looks so itchy, like a Halloween mask that's on too tight and makes you feel like you can't breathe.

"Does Ruby know you have Sensory Processing Disorder?" Maureen asks as she lifts up my right hand and brushes up and down my fingers.

"Of course not!"

"But she's your best friend," Maureen says. "Why wouldn't you tell her?"

I don't respond. If Ruby *really* knew how weird I am, I doubt she'd be my friend. In preschool or even in my first few years at The Children's School, I wasn't exactly popular. I think on some level I was always that girl who threw her sneakers at the audience during the preschool Christmas performance.

"Do you think Ruby is perfect?" Maureen asks, brushing my other hand. "Don't you think she has problems too?"

I glance at Maureen and then look away. I'm relieved she doesn't force me to make eye contact. I hate when adults say *look at me when I'm talking to you*. They don't realize that sometimes eye contact actually hurts.

"Ruby might have problems," I finally say, "but mostly she's pretty normal."

"Define normal," Maureen says.

"It's . . ." I pause, trying to come up with the right words. "*Normal*. You know . . . people who aren't weird. People who know the right things to say and people who play soccer like it's easy and people who don't have to be told to settle down all the time."

"You'd be surprised," Maureen says, "at all the different ways there are of being a person, and also what people privately struggle with. Life isn't always easy. Not for anyone."

I shrug. "I guess."

"I know," Maureen confirms.

On my way out the door Maureen gives me another piece of Hubba Bubba. I chew it the whole way home, until it's long out of flavor.

CHAPTER 12

Ruby still isn't at school on Tuesday. That evening, Dad tells me that Ruby is finally feeling better and he suggests that I call her or use his phone to text her.

"Why?" I ask. I'm sitting at the kitchen table working on my reading response that Ms. Lacey assigned for tomorrow.

"I just thought it would be nice to break the ice before you see each other tomorrow morning," Dad says. "We've told you kids some really big news, and we know it's going to have an impact on your friendship. It might be helpful to talk for a bit. Sandhya and I would even be happy to be on the call. We could do it on speakerphone."

"Yeah, no thanks on that," I say without looking up from my homework.

I can feel Dad standing above me for a long moment before he sighs heavily and heads into the living room.

What Dad doesn't understand is that I have no idea what I'd say to Ruby on the phone. Whenever I think about our parents getting married, how they're going to be sleeping in the same bed and Ruby's going to be living in our apartment, I feel wiggly and terrible, like I can hardly stand being in my own body. Even though the temperature has been cool this week, I haven't been able to wear jeans or leggings for even a millisecond. As soon as I pull them on, I immediately yelp and shiver and kick them off my legs.

So that's why, when Ruby walks into the classroom on Wednesday morning, I feel so nervous I practically slip out of my chair. The only reason I don't is because I can feel Avery watching me. But just as I'm kicking my legs and jiggling my wrists and wondering how I'm going to hold still enough to stay out of the Think Chair today, Ruby heads right over to me and hands me a large yellow envelope. Her hair is back in a ponytail and she's wearing her Manchester United soccer shirt. She's biting her bottom lip and she looks pretty nervous.

"For me?" I ask.

Ruby nods tentatively.

"Should I open it now?"

Ruby's tongue flicks to where her palate expander used to be. "If you want to."

I glance around the classroom. Avery is still watching us. I turn my back so she can't spy and then rip at the envelope, pulling out the paper inside. As soon as I see it, I can't help smiling. Ruby has drawn me a dog picture with pugs and retrievers and even what looks like a massive Bernese mountain dog.

"I went to a website to figure out how to draw that one," she says, pointing to the mountain dog. "I hope it doesn't look like a poop explosion. Also, I wrote you a note on the other side."

"I could tell right away it's a Bernese mountain dog," I say. "Definitely not a poop explosion."

I'm still smiling when I turn over the paper.

Dear Willa,

I know it's weird that my mom and your dad are getting married, but I just wanted to say that we will be friends no matter what.

Your BFF and soon-to-be stepsister,
Rubes

"Did your mom tell you to do this to break the ice?" I ask Ruby.

"No," Ruby says, looking down at her hands. "I just wanted to . . . my mom said that . . ."

Just then, Avery wanders over. I quickly shove the paper back into the envelope.

"Hey, Ruby," Avery says. "Did you know we have a reading response due today? Also, do you want to copy my notes from Monday and Tuesday so you don't fall behind? I doubt you can read Willa's messy handwriting."

I glare at Avery. It's not my fault I have messy handwriting! I could barely hold a pencil until I was six.

"That's okay," Ruby says. "I'll ask Ms. Lacey for the notes."

But instead of talking to the teacher, Ruby grabs the bathroom pass and hurries out the door. As soon as she's gone, Avery stares down at my bare shins. "Shorts again?" she asks. "And why do you have so many bruises on your legs?"

"None of your business!" I snap.

I open my book and refuse to look up until eventually Avery drifts back to her seat. After a few minutes, Ruby returns to the classroom and slides into her table spot. I tear a piece of paper out of my notebook, tuck it inside my book, and pluck a pencil from the jar on the shelf.

Dear Ruby,

Thank you for the drawing. I love it. I'm sorry I said that about breaking the ice.

Your BFF,
Willa

PS I'm sorry again. I guess I'm feeling a little confused about everything.

I don't write anything about the marriage or soon-to-be stepsisters. Instead I draw a soccer ball and goals and I even write *Manchester United rocks* on the bottom before folding the paper and pushing it across the table to Ruby. She smiles as she reads it. I smile back at her. I hope things are okay again. Maybe not *forever okay* because I know that's not going to happen. But *okay for now* would be fine with me.

....

In the cafeteria a few hours later, I unzip my lunch only to find Benji's ham sandwich and a container of leftover meatballs. Ugh. The only vegetarian thing in his lunch is a slimy yogurt squeeze that I wouldn't eat in a million years.

I groan loudly and rest my head on the sticky table. It smells like a queasy mix of applesauce and antibacterial spray.

"What's wrong?" Ruby asks. She's got a bagel with peanut butter, a bag of pretzels, a box of animal crackers, dried mango strips, and a KIND bar. Ruby's mom makes the best lunches, full of packaged foods that my dad doesn't let us eat. I wonder whether Ruby's mom will pack my lunches when they're married. Then I push that thought far from my head.

"My dad put Benji's containers in my lunch," I tell her.

I don't add that he was probably too distracted being in love with Ruby's mom and texting her every single second to put my containers in my lunch.

"Can't you go upstairs and trade lunches with Benji? I'm sure if you told the cafeteria monitors they'd let you go."

I glance at the clock. "The second graders had lunch an hour ago. Benji's probably eaten it all."

I tug at my bracelets. Maureen let me pick out two blue ones on Monday. I stretch them hard and snap them onto my wrist. I'm starving and when I'm starving I become *hangry*. That's what my mom calls it. *Hungry* and *angry* mixed together. Bad combination.

"Here," Ruby says, offering me half her bagel. "You can have this."

I glance down at the bagel in her hand. It's cinnamon-raisin, my favorite. "Really?"

"Definitely," Ruby says. "No need for you to get hangry. That's what my mom calls it when I'm hungry and angry."

"Mine says the same thing!" I say, grinning.

We smile at each other and I suddenly remember why Ruby and I became friends. Even though there are so many ways we're different, there are a lot of ways we click too. I've been forgetting that these past few weeks.

"You pick," Ruby says, holding up her animal crackers and the pretzels. "I'll have one and you have the other. And we can split the dried mango and the KIND bar."

"Are you sure?" I ask, checking out the flavor on the KIND bar. Salted caramel. Yum. "You can have some of Benji's food if you want. He has a ham sandwich and meatballs."

"That's okay," Ruby says. "I have plenty. My mom always sends too much."

I pull open the pretzels and lick the salt off a few pieces and then eat the bagel half and help myself to a mango slice.

"I have to admit something to you," Ruby says after a few minutes. "My mom actually *did* tell me to break the ice. She used those exact words. That's why I made you that picture."

"My dad said the same thing," I say quietly. "Break the ice."

"They must have talked."

"Only twenty times a day!" I say.

"More like fifty! My mom stayed home with me on Monday, and they were calling and texting constantly."

"It's so gross," I say.

"Okay, I'll admit that the constant texting and talking is getting a little gross," Ruby says. "And agreeing to tell us the same things, like to 'break the ice.' We'll have to be sure to call them on it when they do things like that. But can you admit it's ten percent cute?"

"No way. One hundred percent gross."

I'm about to tell Ruby what I've been thinking about these past few days, about how if she had sided with me against our parents' relationship then maybe they wouldn't have decided to get engaged. But as I nibble another mango slice I wonder if maybe she actually *wants* them to be together, if she likes it. It sort of feels like she does. And if I want to be a good friend to her right now—just like how she's being a good friend by sharing her lunch—then I should hush up for a minute about how much I hate the whole situation.

"Ready?" I ask Ruby as everyone starts packing up their lunches and heading toward the doors that lead to the recess yard.

"Yeah." But then she glances nervously at the cafeteria monitors before adding, "Except I really have to—"

"Pee?" I ask.

"How did you know?"

I smile. "We're best friends, remember?"

"I just hate how the monitors always yell at the people who go to the bathroom and tell them to hurry up."

"Come on," I say, standing up and offering Ruby my hand. "I'll go with you. Let them yell at me."

Ruby clutches her lunch in one hand and my hand in the other, and we walk across the cafeteria and into the bathroom.

CHAPTER 13

As soon as I get home that afternoon, I run into my room and call my mom. I'm totally freaking out. I just checked the mail and my middle school letter arrived!

"Hey, Willa," Mom says. "I'm walking into a class. Is everything okay?"

"I got into Maya Angelou!" I shout.

"Honey, that's wonderful!" Mom says. "Wow! Have you told Dad yet?"

"No, I called you first."

If I could write a manual for divorced parents, I would explain that they should never ask their kids that question, because no matter what it's going to make the kid feel guilty, like they're being forced to admit they picked one parent over the other.

"Wow," Mom says again. "That's amazing. Maya A. is one of the best middle schools in the city."

"I'm nervous," I say, gathering my hair into a ponytail. "It's supposed to be really hard. Tons of homework."

"I know you can handle it," Mom says. "Maya A. only lets in kids who they think are up to the challenge."

I drag my hands through my LEGO bin, picking up fistfuls and letting them waterfall down my arms. Maybe Mom is right, but it's still scary. Last fall, we toured middle schools and we ranked my choices and I took the entrance test. Everything seemed to be about getting into a good school. Until this moment it never felt real that I'd actually have to go somewhere new.

"I'm proud of you," Mom says. "It's a huge accomplishment."

"Thanks," I say.

"Have you thought any more about what we talked about last weekend? About the possibility of you coming up here for middle school? Because even though you got into Maya A., that is still on the table as well."

My ponytail suddenly feels too tight. I hook my finger inside the rubber band and attempt to wriggle it off, but it gets stuck and I have to rip it out, pulling a bunch of hair with it.

"Dad agrees it could be a good idea," Mom continues, "a chance for you to spend time with me and also to have less of the sensory input of—"

"I have to tell Dad about Maya A.," I say, cutting her off. "Bye! Talk to you later." I hang up and then hit my dad's name.

"I got into Maya Angelou!" I announce as soon as he answers.

"Honey, that's wonderful," Dad says. "They said the letters were coming this week. Congratulations!"

"I told Mom already," I tell him so he doesn't ask.

"I can't believe you're going to middle school," he says.

I donkey kick my feet behind me. "Do you know if Ruby got her letter?"

"Not yet," Dad says. "Sandhya's at work and Ruby's still at afterschool."

Of course Dad would know about Ruby's letter because he and Ruby's mom have probably been texting every time they have a bite of food or a sip of water.

"I just wanted you to know," I say. "I've got to go."

For the second time in five minutes I push END as quickly as I possibly can.

"I'm so proud of you," Dad says when he gets home that night.

Joshua comes out of the kitchen, where he's been mashing guacamole and steaming rice. Often my dad will text him when he's on the way home and ask him to start dinner. "It's amazing news about Willa, right?" Joshua says.

I hold up the letter so Dad can see MAYA ANGELOU MIDDLE SCHOOL right there on the paper.

"Dad!" Benji shouts, running across the apartment and pummeling into my dad. "I have to show you the new

Pokémon cards I got! Joshua took me to that dollar store on Broadway."

My dad hangs his bag over a doorknob and leans down to unlace his shoes. "First let me take off my shoes and wash my hands. Then we'll do some looking and reading."

Joshua sets a timer for the rice and waves good-bye. We all shout that we'll see him tomorrow. I like that about Joshua. We've had sitters who linger and chat when my dad gets home, but Joshua leaves right away. It's not that I don't like Joshua being here, because I do. But he also understands that we want our dad to ourselves now.

Once we're on the couch, Benji on one side and me on the other, Dad reads my middle school letter and admires Benji's Pokémon cards, and then he wraps us both into a hug. These are the moments I love, Dad and Benji and me together and no one else around.

"By the way," I say, wrinkling my nose at my dad, "thanks for giving me Benji's lunch today. Ham sandwich and meatballs. Yuck. And by thanks I mean no thanks."

"Oh no!" Dad slaps his forehead with his palm. "I'm so sorry, Willa."

"Don't yuck my yum," Benji says. Then he laughs and adds, "But I have to admit your peanut butter and honey sandwich was yummy. So were the apple slices sprinkled with cinnamon. Can I have that tomorrow, Dad?"

"Thanks a lot for eating my lunch," I grumble.

Dad apologizes again and explains how he got an important call as he was making our lunches last night. I wonder if the important call was from Ruby's mom.

"So what did you do for lunch?" he asks. "Were you able to get school lunch?"

I make a face. I can't believe Dad doesn't know by now that school lunch is inedible. Seriously, it's like they scoop up rotten compost and dump it onto a tray.

"Ruby gave me half her bagel," I say, "and a bag of pretzels. And some of her salted caramel KIND bar."

"Lucky!" Benji calls out. My dad never buys those for us because he says they have too much sugar. "And also that's not fair."

"You think it's fair that you ate my lunch? The least I could do was have half a KIND bar."

"Speaking of Ruby," Dad says to me, "Sandhya called a few minutes ago. Ruby got into Maya Angelou as well!"

I wonder if Ruby's mom called as Dad was walking from the subway or even riding the elevator up to our apartment. I wonder if they said *I love you* as they were hanging up. Yuck. No yum whatsoever.

"That's great about Ruby," I finally say.

Maya A. was Ruby's top choice too. This whole year we've been saying how we want to go to middle school together. Even a few weeks ago, that seemed like the most important thing in the world, to be together with Ruby all day long.

"Our smart girls," Dad says, pulling me into another hug.

"We're not *our*," I say, wriggling away from him and hopping onto the trampoline. "We're yours and hers."

"Technically," Benji says, "since Dad and Sandhya are engaged, then yours and hers make ours."

I roll my eyes at my brother. Dad's phone dings in his pocket. He pulls it out and glances at the screen.

"It's a text from Mom," he says to me. "She's out of her class and wants to see if you want to do best part worst part."

I shake my head. "You can tell her that my best part and worst part are the same thing. Finding out about middle school."

I leap off the trampoline and go into my room, slamming the door behind me. I slam it so hard that my golden retriever poster falls off the wall. I stick it back up and then dive face-first onto my bed.

....

The next morning at school, it's total chaos. Ms. Lacey doesn't even try to quiet everyone down. The arrival of the middle school letters is all people are talking about. Elijah got into Maya A. and so did a few other girls in our class and some of the LEGO-trading boys. The Robbins twins wanted The Tech School, but they got into Upper West Secondary, and they're fine with it because they'll be together. And

Avery got into the performing arts school in Midtown that she auditioned for and has been talking about nonstop since September.

"Congratulations," I say to her. And I mean it. It's also congratulations to me because this will be the first time since preschool that I don't have to see Avery on a daily basis.

"Thanks, Willa." Avery flips her long hair over her shoulder. "And congrats on getting into Maya A. My dad is taking me to buy a phone after school today. He promised to get me a phone if I got accepted, because I'll have to take the bus there by myself."

"That's great," I say, smiling.

This is probably the first semi-normal conversation Avery and I have had in the eight years we've known each other.

"You don't have a phone yet, do you?" Avery asks.

I shake my head.

"Probably because you lost your backpack three times in second grade," she concludes. "And how many times have you lost your water bottle this year? You have a new one every few weeks."

I glare at Avery. I can't believe I thought we were having a normal conversation! I'm about to tell her that I hope she drops her new phone in the toilet when Ms. Lacey rings the bell for us to gather on the rug.

Later that day, I ditch my backpack on the living room floor and start jumping on the trampoline. Joshua arrives with Benji from his climbing class and makes us cinnamon toast. I nibble half of it and then go into my room to build LEGOs. I can't stop thinking about what Maureen said yesterday when I told her about the possibility of me going to middle school in Tomsville. I thought Maureen would agree that it's a bad idea because I hate change and also because I never want to give up doing occupational therapy with her, but instead she told me that she believes I can handle more than I think. She also told me she sees patients in her gym on Saturdays, so I could have my appointment on the weekend instead.

"So if I lived with my mom from Monday to Friday, I wouldn't have to stop coming to you?" I asked.

Maureen nodded. "If that happens I could still see you every Saturday."

"But not twice a week like now," I pointed out.

"For you, Willa, I would open the gym on Sundays," Maureen said. "But like I've said before, I think you'd be okay scaling back to once a week. There are so many great occupational therapy opportunities near where your mom lives in the Hudson Valley. I have a friend who does OT with horseback riding. I could give your mom the name of the stable."

"I like horses," I said. "Not as much as I like dogs. But it does sound like fun."

I guess that's on my mind as I hide out in my bedroom—the fact that I didn't freak out when I considered the possibility of moving to my mom's from Monday to Friday and going to middle school up there. One plus of living in Tomsville is that I wouldn't have to deal as much with Ruby and her mom living in our apartment after our parents get married. I could almost pretend it didn't happen.

Thinking about this, I suddenly feel incredibly tired. I climb onto my bed, pull my knees to my chest, and close my eyes.

The next thing I know, Dad is sitting on the edge of my bed, smoothing my hair back from my face. I roll over on my pillow and look up at him.

"When did you get home?" I ask.

"Just now." He touches my cheek with his palm. "You must have fallen asleep. Are you feeling okay? Maybe you got what Ruby had."

"I don't feel sick," I say, hugging my stuffed dog. I've had Woofers since I was three. To most people she looks worn and matted, but to me she's just right. "Can you lie with me?"

"Of course," Dad says. He wriggles out of his blazer and heaves himself onto my bed. I have to press myself sideways against the wall for him to fit.

"You won't be able to do this when Ruby lives here," I whisper.

Dad slides his arm under my shoulder. "It will be different but I'm sure I'll be able to lie in bed with you. And I've been thinking about your sticker charts and checklists. We can still do them when Ruby lives here. We'll just keep them on my desk so it's more private."

"But if Ruby and I share the big bedroom then wouldn't it be weird for you to be lying in bed with me? Like with Ruby right there?"

"We'll figure that out," Dad says. "Can you trust me on this one? Sandhya and I are talking about it all the time, who will be in what bedroom and what will work best for everyone."

I run my fingers over my dad's scratchy chin. Usually I need answers about everything, every little detail, but maybe for now I can let myself believe that he'll take care of it.

"If I live with Mom," I ask after a minute, "will you be mad at me?"

Dad rolls over so he's nose to nose with me. His breath smells minty and a bit like coffee too. "Mom and I were talking about the possibility of you going to middle school in Tomsville even before Sandhya and I got engaged, and I know she talked with you last weekend. Of course I wouldn't be mad. Just like Mom hasn't been mad because you've lived with me from Monday to Friday for the past three years."

I rub my fingers around Woofer's nose as my eyes prickle with tears. The thought of not living with Dad during the week makes me sad, but it also makes me sad that I don't get to see Mom every day.

It's all so confusing.

"What do you think I should do?" I ask.

"Of course I'd love for you to be here," Dad says, "but I also think it would be wonderful for you to get to spend more time with Mom. I would miss you but you'd come here every weekend. Just like how you go to Tomsville now. And I'd come up for all the important events at your school just like how Mom does now."

"What about Benji?" I ask. Even though my little brother drives me crazy I can't imagine being apart from him. "Would he move too?"

"I'm not sure," Dad says, sighing. "He still has three years left at The Children's School."

"I hate divorce," I blurt out. I'm not trying to be mean, but it's true. Everything would be easier if my parents were together and we didn't have to think about all these decisions, all these constant changes.

"Me too," Dad says, sighing heavily.

"You do?" I ask. "But then you wouldn't be together with Ruby's mom."

"I love Sandhya . . . but it's also sad. I know that. In a perfect world, parents stay together and no one has to go through this. But it's not a perfect world. No one is perfect. Things happen . . . and we have to learn to adjust."

Just then, Benji barges into my bedroom. He's holding his flag book, which he's been reading obsessively since Bill gave it to him last weekend. "Did you know that the red, white,

146

and red on the flag of Austria comes from Duke Leopold's white coat being drenched with blood during a battle?" My brother halts when he notices we're on my bed. "Hang on, is Willa sick? Is she going to school tomorrow?"

"No, no, and yes," my dad says, laughing. "And try to remember to knock next time."

"Yes, she's going to school?" Benji asks. "And sorry about not knocking . . . I just couldn't believe that fact about the flag of Austria."

"Do people at school ever make fun of you?" I ask. "For all the facts you know?"

"Not really." Benji shakes his head. "It's just who I am. Hang on, Dad—is Willa staying home sick tomorrow?"

"Yes, she's going to school," my dad says, "and no, she's not sick. And no, I didn't know that about the Austrian flag."

"Supposedly the white was where the duke had his belt on. That was the only place that didn't get soaked in blood."

"Gross," I say, groaning.

"It's just a legend," Benji says, wandering back into the living room, "but I believe it."

I wait until Benji is out of earshot and then whisper, "What about how I lose my water bottle all the time? And what if Mom doesn't pre-stretch my socks in the morning the way you do?"

Dad rests his hand on my arm. "Mom knows who you are and so do I. Your brain is dealing with other things, bigger things than water bottles. And we understand that your sock issues are very real. She's not going to forget about that."

I squirm around in my few inches of space between my dad and the wall. It's so much to think about at once, middle school and where I'll live and my dad and Ruby's mom.

"You don't have to choose between us, Willa," Dad says, squeezing his arms around me. "This is about where you are Monday through Friday and Saturday and Sunday. This isn't about choosing. You have us both."

I try to stop wiggling and settle my body down but it's hard. *It's not a perfect world*, I hear Dad's voice saying to me. I don't have to be perfect. No one's asking me to be. But it's one thing to know that and it's another to feel it deep in my body.

CHAPTER 14

The next week is a really good week. Maybe for some people a good week is a surprise trip to Disney World or a shopping spree or a pop-music concert. But for me I just like it when people are nice and there are no bumps in the road. On Monday, I remembered to bring in two Race Car Driver minifigures to give to Sophie in exchange for the LEGO dog she gave to me. The minifigure gifts made her so excited I thought she might actually talk. Instead she gave me a huge smile and bounced up and down in her chair. Also things with Ruby are good. We haven't discussed our parents at all, and they haven't planned any last-minute dinners or meet-ups, so it almost feels like we're back to our regular friendship. On top of that, the weather has gotten warm and I've been able to wear shorts every day without freezing my legs off, and I've had several comfy sock mornings in a row.

No bumps in the road. No bumps in my socks.

I'm going to tell Maureen that they should make a T-shirt that says that.

And now, on Thursday morning, our class is starting to plan our end-of-year Field Day, which will be in Central Park. Ms. Lacey is saying how she couldn't possibly have considered going to the park until now, but her allergies have finally settled down. The instant she says that, Avery's hand shoots in the air.

"My mom says the tree-pollen season is better," Avery offers. "I can show you the allergy index on my new phone."

"Thanks, Avery," Ms. Lacey says. "But no phones in the classroom. They stay in your backpack all day."

Avery frowns, obviously disappointed that she's not getting a chance to show off her new phone. It's all she's been bragging about at lunch and recess. She even got a sparkly case that matches her sparkly shoes.

At recess today, Avery smuggles her phone outside in the pocket of her lunch box. She has a group of girls crowded around looking at pictures of her and her sister getting manicures and pedicures. As everyone *oohs* and *aahs* about the pictures of shooting stars painted onto her toenails, I mutter to Ruby, "I can't believe someone would *pay* to get their toenails trimmed. I would pay *not* to have someone touch my toenails."

I slap my hand over my mouth. That thought just floated into my head and I said it before I realized it might sound weird. It's like saying I don't like to wash my hair. Then again, I do hate having my hair washed.

"That mood-changing nail polish Avery had was cool," Ruby says. "I once had a mood ring like that."

I stare at Ruby. We have an unspoken agreement never to side with Avery on anything. "Are you saying you liked Avery's nail polish?"

"Just the mood-changing polish," she says, shrugging. "But, yeah, pedicures sound boring."

"Can you imagine being the mood-changing nail polish on Avery's fingers?"

"It would show a bad mood," Ruby says, kicking a soccer ball against the schoolyard wall.

"Twenty-four hours a day," I say.

The ball rolls back to Ruby and she kicks it again. "Seven days a week. Three hundred sixty-five days a year."

I'm just about to add decades and centuries and millennia when the teachers blow their whistles and recess is over.

....

That evening my dad's phone keeps ringing. Every time it rings he snatches it up and walks into his bedroom, closing the door behind him. By the third call, Benji and I crawl down the hall. Resting on our hands and knees, we press our ears against his bedroom door, but all we can hear are muffled sounds. When Dad finally opens the door, he practically trips over us sprawled out on the floor.

"What is it?" Benji and I demand at the same time.

"What's *what*?" Dad slides his phone into his back pocket. He's doing his best innocent face even though a grin is totally busting through. "I have no idea what you're talking about. And why are you lying there with your ears under the door? Really. So strange."

Laughing, Benji wriggles up my dad's legs and onto his back while I wrap my elbows and knees tight around his right leg.

"It's really strange," Dad says, staggering toward the couch with Benji draped over his back and me attached to his leg like a barnacle. "I feel a little heavy, like there's something on my back and leg. Or maybe my foot just fell asleep while I was on that super boring phone call."

"What phone call?" I shout from the floor.

"Still so strange," Dad says. "I hear voices but I can't tell where they're coming from."

"Here!" Benji and I shout together.

Dad shakes his leg and shimmies his shoulders from side to side, but he's unable to shake Benji and me off. Benji and I are laughing like crazy as Dad finally dumps us onto the couch and then flops between us.

"Okay," he says, exhaling loudly. "I suppose I should tell you. I was on the phone with the woman from Manhattan Mutts."

"Who?" Benji asks.

"The rescue place from Puppapalooza!" I say, springing off the couch and bouncing onto the trampoline.

Dad nods. "I emailed her and we've been going back and forth. She called my references and just had some follow-up questions tonight."

I jump onto one leg and then shift to the other. "What did she say? Did we get approved to adopt a dog?"

"She said we sound like a great family for a rescue dog," Dad says, grinning. "I even made a donation to Manhattan Mutts on the phone tonight, which is required for adopting."

"Oh . . . Daddy! Thank you! I love you!" I'm spinning 360s on the trampoline and waving my arms in the air.

"I love you, too, Waggy," Dad says. "I'm glad your dog dream is finally happening."

"Who did you use as references?" Benji asks. He's still on the couch, his head resting on a pillow and his feet in Dad's lap.

"Mom," Dad says, holding up his thumb as if to tick off one, "because the dog will be going up there whenever you guys do." Then Dad holds up his pointer and says, "And Joshua. He's in our home a lot and he knows we would take good care of a dog."

"That's it?" Benji asks, sitting up and crossing his arms over his chest.

After a brief hesitation Dad holds up a third finger. "And Sandhya. She will be living here, so it will be her dog as well."

At the mention of her name I start bouncing harder on the trampoline, first on my heels and then on my toes.

"Does Sandhya even like dogs?" Benji asks.

I jump in a semicircle but don't take my eyes off Dad. I hadn't even considered the possibility that she wouldn't like dogs.

Dad clears his throat. "Sandhya is on board. She understands that we're getting a dog."

Benji and I wait for him to say more, but he clears his throat again and then pulls his phone out of his back pocket and stares at the screen.

....

Over the weekend, my mom and I finally have a good conversation about me moving in with her during the week. It's not like we say I'm going to or I'm not going to but we're able to talk about it without me flipping out. It's Sunday morning, Mother's Day, and Bill has taken Benji to Mom's favorite bakery to get us cinnamon rolls for breakfast. I'm snuggling in bed with her and telling her about Manhattan Mutts and Field Day and who got into what middle school. I love morning snuggles with my mom. She knows just how to hold me, not so tight that it hurts my skin but not so floppy that I need to be squeezed harder.

"It's scary to think about moving up here for school," I tell her.

"Yes, I know." She reaches across the pillow and runs her fingers through my hair, untangling some curls. Mom doesn't wear her glasses in bed, so it feels like I get a special view of her that the rest of the world doesn't see.

"How would I make friends?" I ask. "I wouldn't know anyone and they'd all know each other."

"It's true that a lot of them would know each other," Mom says, "but the sixth graders would be coming to the middle school from three separate elementary schools. It's the perfect time for you to come because a lot of kids would be meeting for the first time. Also, I'd put you in some local camps. Tomsville Middle School does a LEGO-building camp in July."

I nod. A LEGO-building camp sounds fun. Most camps make you chase and kick and dodge balls for the entire day. Either that or do arts and crafts, which aren't really my thing either.

"Maureen says that change happens whether you want it or not," I tell Mom.

"That's true," she says.

"She also says that sometimes being in a hard place and letting yourself be there is the only way for things to feel better," I say.

Mom nods. "I've definitely felt that way sometimes."

I wonder if she's thinking about when she and Dad got divorced. It was a long time ago but I still remember walking in on her crying a few times.

"Maureen said there's a horse place near here," I say, quickly changing the subject. I didn't mean to make her feel sad on Mother's Day. "Like where I could do occupational therapy if I lived up here."

"She emailed me about that," Mom says, propping her head up on her elbow. "I was thinking we could drive over one weekend and check out the stable. Therapeutic horse-back riding is supposed to be great for people with sensory issues."

"I'd like that," I say, except all of a sudden *I'm* feeling sad, like a rain that comes out of nowhere on a clear spring day. I hug my arms around myself. "What's wrong with me? Will I need to do OT and all this stuff forever?"

"There's nothing wrong with you." Mom wraps her arms around me and pulls me in. Her skin is warm and she smells like coconut body lotion, but not so strong that it's gross. "I see parts of me in you, like how I need routine and solitude and could spend hours in comfy pajamas reading books. And I see parts of Dad in you. He's always in motion, always fidgeting. He loves the noise and chaos of the city and his work and his phone constantly going. Sensory Processing Disorder is not your fault. As you get older, it will become easier to live with, and eventually it'll be some of the most essential parts of what makes you *you*."

"Sort of like how best part worst part makes a whole day?" I ask.

Mom kisses my forehead and then says, "Best part worst part makes a whole day. But you, Willa, are all best parts. Even the things you struggle with." She pauses. "Especially the things you struggle with. That's what makes you unique."

"Or weird," I mutter.

"Unique. Wonderful. Totally Willa."

Ruby and I have struck a careful peace. We are okay as long as we don't talk about our parents getting married and how she thinks it's a good thing and I know it's a terrible thing. It almost feels like we're back to our normal friendship. No one at school—other than Avery—knows that our parents are together, so that makes it easier to pretend it's not happening. I have to admit I'm grateful that Avery isn't rubbing it in on a daily basis. Avery doesn't know about their wedding plans, of course, but I would have thought she'd be taunting me with the information she does have. But I can't let myself get too grateful because I have to be on guard with Avery. There's always that chance she's waiting, like a dog frozen in the seconds before it chases a squirrel, for the right moment to spread my news and maximize the humiliation.

I don't tell Ruby any of this, of course. For one, she might just say it'd be fine for Avery to tell people because it's good news and we can all celebrate together. Or she might call me paranoid. No thanks on either of those.

After school on Tuesday, Joshua takes Ruby, Benji, and me to Central Park to climb rocks. It's the first time we've gotten together outside school since our parents announced their engagement and it actually feels normal. Mostly we don't talk about it, except once, when we're at the top of a tall boulder, Benji tells Ruby that after our parents get married and move in together we should convince them to install climbing holds all over the walls of our apartment. I watch Ruby carefully to see what she'll say but she just shrugs and says, "It's your apartment. You should ask Willa."

That evening, I smooth out Ruby's dog drawing with my palm and then tape it on my wall next to the golden retriever poster. I'd had it stored in my backpack since she gave it to me two weeks ago, but luckily it didn't get too crumpled in there.

On Wednesday afternoon, right before the end of the day, Ms. Lacey calls a class meeting to firm up Field Day details. It's happening in a few weeks. We've decided we're going to go to the Central Park Zoo and then take a bus uptown to a grassy area to meet the other classes and have a picnic.

"I emailed all the parents yesterday to ask for chaperones," Ms. Lacey says. "We have enough for now but if you want your parents to come there's room for everybody. I just need to know in advance so I can get enough tickets for the zoo."

Avery's hand shoots in the air. "My parents can't make it because they're taking a mini-vacation to Cape Cod," she says. "It's their *seventeenth* anniversary."

"Too bad they'll miss it," Ms. Lacey says. "We'll take lots of pictures."

"It's okay," Avery says, shrugging. "My grandma is staying with us and she loves shopping. She'll buy us anything we want." Avery jiggles her charm bracelet on her wrist, showing off two new charms: a tiny silver phone and yet another dog charm.

Norie raises her hand next. "Who is chaperoning Field Day?"

Ms. Lacey reaches into her desk for a piece of paper. I'm only half listening because my parents rarely chaperone field trips. Dad says it's hard to take off the time from work and Mom finds chaperoning overwhelming, especially herding the bad listeners, which is every kid on a field trip. I half hear Ms. Lacey say that Elijah's mom is chaperoning and Norie and Zoe's dad and Haley's aunt. But I quickly tune back in when she finishes with, "And we've also got Willa's dad and Ruby's mom."

No. No. No.

I can't look at Ruby. I can't look at Avery. This definitely can't happen. There's no way my dad and Ruby's mom can chaperone the field trip together. If they do, we'll run the risk of them holding hands or, even worse, kissing and blabbering about how they're getting married. Also if Avery sees them together it'll definitely signal her to tell everyone in the fifth grade about how lovey they looked at that Italian restaurant, and maybe even how she knew before Ruby and me that our parents were together.

As soon as Ms. Lacey dismisses us, I grab my backpack, race down the stairs, and hurry home, where I immediately call my dad.

"You can't chaperone Field Day," I tell him as soon as he picks up.

"Hi to you, too, Waggy," Dad answers. "How was your day? Oh, that's wonderful! So is mine, thanks for asking."

"Please no Dad Jokes," I tell him. "Just tell me you won't chaperone Field Day."

"I always thought you wanted me to chaperone," Dad says. "I figured since it's your last field trip at The Children's School, I'd take the day off and come along."

I don't want to hurt my dad's feelings or invite any nosy questions. "I just want Field Day to be my time," I say vaguely. "No parents."

Dad agrees that he'll email Ms. Lacey, and then he reminds me that he'll be home by six thirty for Taco Bowl Wednesday.

"But you're going out tomorrow night, right?" I ask.

"Yes. Sandhya and I are having dinner. Joshua is staying late and putting you to bed."

I'm so relieved he's not chaperoning Field Day that yet *another* date night with Ruby's mom doesn't bother me too much.

The next morning during quiet reading, Ms. Lacey calls Ruby and me up to her desk. Ruby and I haven't talked since I rushed out of the classroom yesterday so I could run home and call my dad. When I was unpacking my backpack this morning, she gave me a funny look, but I quickly set my water bottle on the table and buried my face in *The Secret of the Unicorn*. My stepdad, Bill, gave me a few Tintin books over the weekend, ones from when he was a kid, and while I like Tintin, I'm obsessed with his dog, Snowy. I think Snowy is a terrier, probably a wire fox. I'm planning to confirm this with Bill when we go up to Tomsville this weekend.

"I got an email from your dad yesterday afternoon," Ms. Lacey says to me before turning to Ruby, "and also from your mom, Ruby. They both backed out of chaperoning Field Day."

Ms. Lacey points to the list on her desk, where *Greg Garrett* and *Sandhya Kapoor* have red lines through their names. I glance covertly at Ruby. Her tongue is playing with her imaginary palate expander.

"Is everything okay?" Ms. Lacey asks, leaning close to us.

"It's fine," I say quickly.

"Yeah," Ruby agrees. "Totally fine."

Ms. Lacey clears her throat. "When your parents let me know they couldn't chaperone they also told me about—"

"No big deal," I say, cutting her off.

"I just wanted to say congratulations," Ms. Lacey says. "It's exciting but it's also a . . . unique situation."

I'm shifting from leg to leg and wriggling my fingers. I glance across the classroom, where Norie and Zoe are flipping through my comic book and *ooh*ing about how Tintin has the cutest crest of red hair. Through it all, Ruby is staring at the floor, completely still.

"In all my years of teaching," Ms. Lacey is saying, "I don't think I've ever had two parents fall—"

"I need to use the bathroom," I blurt out.

"Me too," Ruby says.

"Okay," Ms. Lacey says, eying us closely. "I can see you don't want to talk about it. But before you go to the bathroom, I wanted to let you both know that there is no need to announce the news to the class. Unless, of course, you wanted to?"

"No thanks!" I say quickly.

As soon as Ms. Lacey excuses us, Ruby and I mad dash toward the door, grabbing two bathroom passes on the way.

"That was awful!" I say as soon as we reach the hallway.

"Double-triple awful!" Ruby says. "I hate being called to the teacher's desk. I always feel like I'm about to get in trouble, like I'm going to get sent to the guidance counselor or something."

I shrug. I'm used to that. It was Ms. Lacey offering to tell the class that was double-triple awful to me. "Did you ask your mom to back out of chaperoning?"

Ruby nods. "I texted her as soon as I got out of school. What about you?"

"I called my dad when I got home. That's the last thing we need, having them holding hands and being all lovey in front of everybody." I pause. "Hang on. Why did you ask your mom? I thought you were excited that they're together."

"I thought it would make you upset, having them together at school."

"You did that for me?"

"Yep," Ruby says, nodding.

"Is there anything I can do to thank you?" I ask.

"You can say that our parents being together isn't the worst thing in the whole world." Ruby pauses. "Maybe it's five percent okay?"

I'm about to say *no way* but then I think about how much fun we had at Puppapalooza until Ruby got sick, and how my dad has been whistling happily when he's doing the dishes recently and he doesn't seem as frustrated in the mornings when I can't find anything comfortable to wear. Finally I shrug and say, "How about point zero zero zero one percent?"

Ruby giggles. "It's a start. Now can I go to the bathroom? I actually have to pee."

"Of course you do!" I say.

I wait until she's done and then we sling our arms around each other and walk like that the whole way back to the classroom.

CHAPTER 15

"How's dinner at six?" Joshua asks, peeking into my Girl Cave.

"Sounds good," I say as I press a LEGO into place. If I were a minifigure, I would snap myself right into the middle of my dog kingdom, happily surrounded by LEGO canines.

"What are we having?" I ask.

"Stir-fry," Joshua says. "And brown rice."

"You're making totally veggie stir-fry?" I ask. Joshua knows I'm a vegetarian but I always like to be *sure sure sure* he doesn't slip in fish sauce.

"Of course," Joshua says. "With tofu."

"Yum," I say, smiling.

Once he's gone I click backward on *Old Yeller* and return to the middle. I listen to the story and build LEGOs until Joshua calls me to the table. Dinner with the three of us turns out to be really fun. Joshua looks up "conversation starters" on his phone, and we go around the table answering questions like *What are the three words that best describe you?* and

What's the most useful thing you own? When I get the question *Are you a very organized person?* my brother and Joshua crack up because I'm the opposite of very organized. I stick my tongue out at them, and even though I wasn't trying to be funny, Benji laughs so hard he spews rice across the table.

After dinner, I get in the bath. On my checklist it says I need to take a bath every Sunday, Tuesday, and Thursday—and other nights if I'm sweaty or dirty. I don't love baths but unless I'm in a bad mood I don't fight things that are on my checklist.

As I swirl my hair around in the water and stretch my toes out, I think about how I can mostly fit in the bathtub. I wonder how much longer I'll be able to. I have to bend my neck and knees, but it's nothing like my mom. Sometimes I sit in the bathroom when she's taking a bath, and she has to fold her knees out of the water like two drippy mountains.

I want to stay small enough to fit in the bathtub forever. As soon as I think that thought, I imagine Maureen saying, *If you can't fit, then get a bigger tub. You're just right the way you are.* I guess it's lucky that my dad is an architect. When I'm older I'll have him design a bathroom for me that fits a tub long enough for grown-ups.

After my bath, I towel off and change into my pajamas. When it's just my dad and Benji, I can wear my towel as I walk through the apartment, but if a babysitter is here I bring in my pajamas with me. I guess that's how it'll be when Ruby and her mom live here, no more towel dashes in search of jammies.

I can hear Benji and Joshua laughing in the living room. I get a hairbrush out of the drawer. I can't find my regular plastic one, so I grab the narrow circular one. It's left over from when my mom lived here. I never use it for my hair because it's too bristly, but I keep it around because I like these small reminders that once upon a time my mom and dad and brother and I were an unbroken family.

"What are you guys talking about?" I ask, flopping onto the couch next to my brother.

Joshua holds up the phone for me to see. "He wanted me to look up the weather in Northeast Greenland National Park."

"It's negative-seven degrees in the middle of May!" Benji says, his eyes glimmering. If there's one thing Benji finds even more exciting than geography and history, it's weather. Last year he had fifteen random locations on my dad's phone and he'd monitor them on a daily basis.

I start working at my hair. When it's wet, the curls become ropy, and this circular brush isn't helping. Every time I try to comb out a section, the brush gets stuck and I have to yank hard to get it out.

"Did you hear the news?" Benji says, glancing up from the weather reports on Joshua's phone.

"What news?" I smudge my finger on the water droplets on my pajamas. They must have fallen from my hair. Now I'm going to have to change my pajamas before bed. No way will I be able to fall asleep with wet pajamas.

"When you were taking a bath," Benji says, "Joshua told me his big news."

I groan and roll my eyes. "Please tell me you're not getting married too."

Joshua laughs so hard he starts to gag. For as long as he's been babysitting us, he's had a boyfriend named Noah. We've met Noah a few times, and he seems nice. But I'm definitely not ready to hear about any more people getting married!

"Nope," Joshua says, catching his breath. "No marriage plans. Noah and I want to wait until we're thirty. The big news is that I got into law school. I'm starting in the fall."

I let out a long breath. "That's great," I say. "It'll be like how you took college classes last fall."

Joshua shakes his head. "Not really . . . because this law school is in Chicago."

I twirl the brush around in my hair. I'm starting to think that I'm not going to like where this big news is going.

Joshua clears his throat. "Noah and I are moving to Chicago in early August to get settled into an apartment. I'll finish up here at the end of July. Right before your dad takes you guys to Vermont."

"There's a great ninja academy in Chicago," Benji offers.

I can't believe this. I can't believe that on top of leaving my school and my dad getting married and Ruby and her mom moving in, we are also losing our sitter! Benji and I have had other sitters in the past—people who were impatient with us or were constantly on their phones—and so we know for a fact that Joshua is the best.

Joshua sets his phone on the coffee table. "Are you okay?"

I shrug like *whatever* because I'm not going to cry in front of Joshua. But then a wave of horror shoots up my spine.

"It's stuck!" I cry out.

"What's stuck?" Joshua asks.

"Ow! Ow! Ow!" I shout, yanking at the brush. But the more I pull, the deeper it gets burrowed in my hair. My wet curls are tangled around the bristles, and my skull is prickling in pain.

"Willa," Joshua says evenly, "can you take a deep breath and let me look at it?"

"I don't want to take a deep breath!" I yell, even though I know it's not his fault, getting the brush stuck or even going to law school in Chicago. But the brush is hurting so much I'm having a hard time keeping my voice calm. "Can you call my dad? Can you ask him to come home?"

"He's at dinner with Sandhya," Joshua says. "Let me give it a try first."

Joshua lifts my hair off my shoulder and reaches in for the brush. But as soon as his hand comes near it, I lurch backward.

"Wow," says Joshua. "That brush is really stuck."

As Joshua wiggles at the brush and Benji fetches a pair of scissors, I start crying, tears and runny nose and hiccuping and all.

"Can you please call my dad?" I ask again. "Or text him?"

Finally, Joshua agrees to text. I watch as he types, **Willa got a brush stuck in her hair and she's really upset.**

"You should say she's crying," Benji offers, but Joshua sends it as is.

"Did he write back?" I whimper. My hand is clutching the side of my head where the brush is twisted and trapped deep in a tangle of my hair.

"It's only been two minutes," Joshua says, glancing down at his phone. "I can try him again. Maybe he didn't hear the text."

After three more minutes with no reply from my dad, I ask Joshua to call my mom.

"Are you sure you don't want me to take another look?"

"No!" I shout, shielding my hand over the hairbrush, which is yanking my hair harder and harder by the second.

"We should just cut it out," Benji says. He's on the couch next to me, holding out the scissors.

"No!" I scream, tears running down my face.

Joshua calls my mom but it goes straight to voicemail. I tell him to call Bill next. Bill answers on the second ring. He tells Joshua that Mom is in a meeting with her phone off and won't be home until nine. Bill offers to drive over and interrupt the meeting, but I tell Joshua to tell Bill that he doesn't have to.

"Do we have to cut it out?" I ask, feeling like we've used up all our options. I'm already imagining how embarrassing it will be to walk into school tomorrow with a chunk of hair missing. Of course Avery will be the first to notice, and of course she'll say that she'd never be stupid enough to get a brush stuck in her hair. Maybe I'll have to wear a hat for the rest of the school year to cover the bald patch. Except I hate hats! Too tight around my head.

Joshua's phone pings. He glances at the text, his shoulders sagging in relief.

"It's your dad," he says. "He and Sandhya have jumped in a taxi. They're on their way."

I slump backward on the couch. I'm too upset by this point to complain that Ruby's mom is going to see me like this. Joshua hands me a tissue and then distracts me by looking up cute dog memes until the front door unlocks.

The second my dad walks in I start crying all over again. He strides quickly across the living room and reaches into my hair, feeling around for the brush.

"Oh, Waggy," Dad says, "it's really stuck. We may have to cut it out."

"That's what I've been saying all along!" Benji says, gesturing to the scissors.

"I'm so sorry," Joshua says. "She was brushing her hair and I was telling her about—"

"Hang on," Ruby's mom says. For the first time I notice her standing behind my dad. She's wearing a pink suit and heels and she's holding a plastic bag from Walgreens. "We stopped by the store and bought some thick conditioner," she explains to me. "Let me give it a try before you resort to scissors. If it's okay with you, of course."

I wipe at my eyes with a tissue. "I guess," I say, sniffling. "I mean, if you think it will help."

Ruby's mom and I walk together into the bathroom, closing the door behind us. She sits me on the toilet lid and hovers above me, squirting conditioner into her hands and carefully weaving her fingers around, sorting through the strands of hair. The whole time she's working she's reassuring me that the brush is coming out, slowly but surely, slowly but surely. As I listen to her voice and feel her fingers in my hair, it's actually relaxing, sort of like when my mom braids my hair.

A few minutes later, she holds up the brush triumphantly in her hand. "It's out!"

I reach up to my hair. My scalp is sore but otherwise everything feels normal.

Sandhya smiles at me. "You, my dear, have beautiful hair. We had to at least *try* to save it."

"Thank you," I say. "Really."

Sandhya drapes a towel over my shoulders and instructs me to lean my head over the sink so she can rinse out the conditioner. When she's done she wraps my hair in a fresh white towel, pats my shoulders, and says, "Let's tell the guys the good news and get you some dry pajamas."

I reach up to make sure the towel is twisted tight around my head and then follow Sandhya into the living room.

"You got it out!" Dad says, standing up from the couch and hugging us both. Joshua must have gone home and Benji is in his bedroom.

"Go change into new pajamas," Sandhya says, handing the brush to my dad, "and I'll meet you in your room to dry your hair."

I nod at her. She's in total mom mode right now, and I'm actually okay with it.

I go into my Girl Cave and change into my striped pajamas. I've had them since I was eight and they're way too short but so soft and comfortable. A few minutes later, Sandhya comes in and glances around my room. I can see her eyes lingering on the golden retriever poster by the door and the dog picture that Ruby drew for me a few weeks ago.

"Your room is so cozy," she says, reaching for the towel on my head. "It's totally you."

"Thanks." I tug at the bracelets on my wrist. "Are you going to tell Ruby about the hairbrush getting stuck?"

Sandhya shakes her head. "Not if you don't want me to." She finishes rubbing my wet hair and then drapes the towel over her arm. "I realize your dad and me being together and then getting engaged is a huge shock. It's a big life change even without the fact that I'm Ruby's mom. And I know it's changing you and Ruby's relationship, like who you are as friends versus who you will be as stepsisters. I realize it's not easy. Your dad and I are asking a lot of you both, and of Benji, too, and we know it may be rocky sometimes."

I nod at Sandhya. She's putting into words exactly what's been on my mind. Also, I like how she's talking to me as an equal, not a little kid who needs to be told that everything will be okay.

"Believe me," Sandhya says, "it's on Ruby's mind too."

"But she always says she's so happy about it. Like it's one hundred percent wonderful that you guys are getting married. I'm sorry for not being totally happy . . . it's just . . ." I try to think of a way to finish my thought but nothing is coming to me.

"Ruby's excited," Sandhya says, "but that doesn't mean she's not also nervous. She's got some things she's really worried about."

I watch Sandhya, wondering if she's going to say anything else about Ruby, but she just tells me she's going to make my dessert, so I should meet her in the kitchen in a few minutes. As she walks out of my room, I blurt out, "I'm sorry I made you leave dinner to come here."

Sandhya pauses in the doorway. "Oh, Willa. Of course we came. As soon as your dad saw the text, we paid and jumped in a car."

I smile at her, realizing that I'm okay with the *we* business. Actually, I kind of like it.

CHAPTER 16

On Monday morning, I'm building with Sophie when there's a knock at the door and Mr. Torres steps into the hallway. As soon as we're alone, Sophie leans across the LEGO-filled table, opens her eyes wide, and whispers, "I hate kindergarten. I cry every day before school but my mom makes me come."

I stare at her little face, unsure what to say. She barely talks and now *this*. I glance around the office at the posters to see if she's reciting a caption, even though I would bet all my LEGOS that Mr. Torres doesn't have a poster that announces, *I cry every day before school but my mom makes me come.* My eyes pause on a poster of an ocean with a quote that says, IN ORDER TO DISCOVER NEW LANDS, ONE MUST BE WILLING TO LOSE SIGHT OF THE SHORE FOR A VERY LONG TIME. I stare at the choppy gray waves, at those words, but then I remember that Sophie is waiting for me to respond.

I realize I can go two ways. I can tell Sophie what adults have said to me over the years, that it'll be okay, that it's probably not as bad as I think, that this, too, shall pass. Or I could tell her the truth.

"I hated kindergarten, too," I say. "It was horrible. Kids were so mean."

As Sophie watches me closely, I think about how even though kindergarten was bad, elementary school slowly got better. It helped a lot to meet Ruby. We're getting excited about fifth-grade graduation in a few weeks. Since Ruby doesn't wear dresses, she suggested we get matching shirts and pants, but I quickly shook my head. The only pants I wear are leggings and a certain stretchy-style pair of jeans. But even with those it has to be a special brand with loose elastic and good seams. I didn't tell Ruby all this. I just said I was planning to wear a dress but maybe we could do matching colors.

"I can't guarantee it'll get better by the time you're in fifth grade," I say to Sophie, "but it did for me and I bet it will for you too."

"How old are you?" Sophie asks.

"Eleven."

"I wish I were eleven. I'm five but they call me a baby. Some kids even try to carry me around. It's not my fault I'm small. It's not my fault my birthday is in December. A lot of people in my class are already six."

"You're definitely not a baby," I tell her. "But it's still not kind of them to call you one."

Sophie smiles shyly and then goes back to not talking for the rest of the session.

That afternoon, after school lets out, I go to the basement to fill my water bottle. The water in the fountain down there is the coldest and tastes the best. I was planning to hide out at the pharmacy like I usually do before my appointment with Maureen, but then I see Ruby walking out of the basement bathroom and heading over to join the other afterschool kids. They're lined up along the walls, their backpacks flung at their feet, eating snacks before their activities start.

I wave at Ruby. I'm about to walk toward the stairs leading to the lobby, but then I notice her shoulders are curved in and she's frowning.

"Are you okay?" I ask.

She squints her eyes and bites at her bottom lip. Ruby only makes this face when she's really upset.

"What's wrong?" I ask.

Ruby sits down around the corner from the noisy pack of afterschool kids and tosses her bag next to her. I glance at the afterschool coaches to see if they're going to tell me I'm supposed to be dismissed already, but they don't seem to notice me. I slide down next to Ruby and hug my backpack against my chest.

"I guess I'm upset about graduation," Ruby says, unzipping her soccer bag and then zipping it up again. "A lot of kids were talking about it just now and I got nervous. I hate being onstage. Also my dad offered to fly in from Michigan, but I said it'd probably make me more nervous to have him here. But now I feel bad that he's not coming. He doesn't come to a lot of my stuff. That's kind of the way he is."

Ruby rarely talks about her dad. I had no idea that he doesn't come to her things, and also I didn't know she was nervous about graduation. I'm trying to figure out the right thing to say when an afterschool coach walks over with the snack basket. It reminds me of a flight attendant on a plane. Ruby reaches in and fishes out a pack of shortbread cookies.

"Want a snack?" the woman asks me. I see her in the halls sometimes and I think her name is Lila. "It's fine if you take something."

I reach in and pick out a chocolate–peanut butter KIND bar. Benji is going to be so jealous when I tell him.

"My mom says that graduation will be okay," Ruby says, unwrapping her cookies. "She says that my dad and I can celebrate in Michigan this summer. And she says that stage fright is normal, lots of people have it. But what if I have to pee in the middle of graduation?" Ruby giggles and then covers her mouth with her hand. "If you can believe it, I have to pee even more when I'm nervous."

I nibble on my KIND bar. "Your mom is really nice," I say. I'm thinking about how she got the brush out of my hair and didn't make me feel bad for getting it stuck. Also, when she said good-bye the other night, she gave me a hug and said she was proud of me.

"She is," Ruby says. I feel her glancing curiously at me, almost like she knows more.

"Did she tell you?" I ask.

"Tell me what?"

"About last week? When they had to leave their dinner early and come over to my apartment. Did she tell you about that?"

"Willa," Ruby says, crumpling the wrapper in her hand. "I have no idea what you're talking about."

I exhale slowly. "It's really embarrassing."

Ruby unzips her soccer bag and digs around, fishing out a spiral notebook and a pencil. "Here," she says, turning to a fresh sheet of paper. "Write it down. Sometimes things are too embarrassing to say out loud."

I nod, clenching the KIND bar between my teeth and balancing the notebook on my knees, and then I write: *I got a hairbrush stuck in my hair and your mom helped get it out. It was really bad.*

"Oh," Ruby says, glancing at what I wrote. "No big deal. My mom is the queen of hair crises. My whole class got lice in second grade. She offered to work on all the kids. She went over to about ten people's houses and helped comb out lice."

"Gross!" I say, instinctively itching at my scalp.

Ruby itches her hair too. "I know."

"But also really nice."

"I know," Ruby says. Then she pauses before adding, "Did your dad tell you?"

"Tell me what?"

Ruby shakes her head and presses her lips together, and so I pass the notebook and pencil over to her. After a moment, I watch her write: *I got lost in a crowd and started crying really hard, and your dad found me.*

"When?" I ask. My dad said that he and Sandhya and Ruby went to the High Line last weekend, which is an elevated train track that the city turned into a park, but he didn't say anything about Ruby getting lost. "You mean at the High Line?"

Ruby nods and then writes down, *It's lucky your dad is tall. He saw me in the crowd and then I saw him waving. I didn't have my phone. I thought I was lost forever.*

I reach over and hug Ruby's shoulder, pulling her in. "My dad is very tall," I say.

"I know," she says. "He's also really understanding. He said it was no big deal that I was crying."

"Ruby!" the afterschool coach Lila shouts down the hall. "Almost ready for soccer? We're heading to the yard in two minutes."

"Okay," Ruby calls back to her. And then, to me, she says, "I have an idea."

"What?"

Ruby tears the page of the notebook and folds it in half

lengthwise, rubbing along the crease. Then she carefully rips the paper in half, handing one side to me.

"You keep half of my secret," Ruby says as she tucks her piece into the small pocket in her bag, "I'll keep half of yours."

"Just like how our parents kept our secrets?"

Ruby nods. "To remember."

"To remember," I agree, nodding. I slide my piece of paper into the cover of my Tintin book because I know I won't lose it there.

Ruby hops up to join the afterschool kids. I take a sip of cold water and then walk out of school and over to my appointment with Maureen.

....

On Thursday afternoon, Sandhya takes me shopping for my fifth-grade graduation dress. She and Dad planned the outing. They even looped Mom into the text chain so she could suggest brands with soft fabrics that have worked for me in the past. I have to admit I liked seeing Mom and Sandhya texting and sending links for clothing sites back and forth. It made me feel like they're going to get along and maybe even become friends someday. I know that sounds strange but it wouldn't be the worst thing ever.

While Sandhya and I are shopping, Benji is staying home with Joshua and my dad is picking Ruby up from afterschool.

For dinner my dad is taking Benji and Ruby to Shake Shack for cheeseburgers and then back to our apartment to do homework. It's a plan that I never would have dreamed up two months ago, but since Sandhya got the brush out of my hair, I've been feeling better about her. Also, I like the thought of my dad being the one to find Ruby when she was lost in a crowd. As soon as I got home from Maureen's on Monday, I took my torn half of the paper out of the Tintin book and put it in the drawer of my bedside table. I've taken it out a few times and looked at it, and it always makes me feel good that we have each other's secrets and our parents do too.

I'm actually excited for our excursion today. After dress shopping, Sandhya is taking me to a vegan fast-food restaurant that she read about. I looked up the menu and they have vegan nachos. And I'll never say no to nachos!

At four, Sandhya meets me at my apartment and we take the subway downtown. On the train, she tells me how she planned a walking route that passes a bunch of clothing stores and ends up at Green Place, the vegan restaurant. But the crazy thing is, at the first store, the third dress I try on is perfect. It's red with purple polka dots. No terrible sleeves that tickle the inside of my arms. Just wide straps that rest on my shoulders and a swirly skirt that puffs out without being itchy.

"I can't believe it," I tell Sandhya as I come out of the dressing room and twirl in a circle.

I *really* can't believe it. Usually shopping involves trying on twenty things with no luck and eventually going home and ordering clothes online and then sending those back because they're terrible too.

"It's comfortable?" Sandhya asks, rubbing the skirt's fabric between her fingers and thumb. I notice a diamond ring on her finger that I'm guessing is an engagement ring from my dad. "It feels soft."

"It's really comfortable," I tell her.

I'm glad we're just saying *comfortable* instead of her asking me specific questions about seams and too-tight squeezes versus just-right squeezes. I know Mom and Dad filled her in on how seams and I don't get along, but it's not like I want to start discussing my sensory stuff with her.

"Yeah," I say, nodding. "It's great. I love it."

"And it's the right colors," Sandhya says. "Red and purple."

I grin. "Exactly."

Those are the colors that Ruby and I decided on. Red for Ruby, of course, and I picked purple. I like how purple is one of the regular colors but also it's unique. On the rainbow it's not even called purple, but it's a mix of indigo and violet. Also Benji told me that for centuries purple has been associated with royalty and power, which sounds fine by me.

"I bought a red blouse for Ruby," Sandhya says. "Now we need to find purple pants and we'll be all set."

I change back into my shorts and T-shirt, and then we go to the register to pay for the dress. I can see the saleswoman studying us like she's trying to determine if we're mother and daughter and, if so, how a petite Indian woman and a tall curly-haired white girl are related. I think about how Ruby hates when people say, *Where are your parents from?* like they're never content with her saying Michigan, like the fact that she doesn't have white skin makes people question her heritage. If anyone ever asks if Sandhya is my mom I'll simply say yes and let them be confused.

Sandhya carries the shopping bag as we meander down Fifth Avenue, looking in store windows. We pass a pet store. Sandhya takes a picture of some plaid doggie beds and we text it to my dad. I point out a candy shop that's famous for their selection of gummies—gummy worms, gummy bears, even gummy dogs!

"We should bring Ruby," I tell her.

"Definitely," Sandhya says. "Before she gets her braces on."

When we get to the vegan restaurant, it's crowded even though it's only five fifteen. We order nachos for me, a Thai salad for Sandhya, and artichoke dip to share. Sandhya even lets me order ginger lemonade. I decide not to tell her that Dad never says yes to sweet drinks in restaurants.

As we're waiting for the food, I go to the bathroom to wash my hands. The walls are covered with pictures of dancing vegetables and they have the loudest hand dryer. It feels amazing on my hands and in my ears too. I hold my fingers under the dryer for a while and then skip happily across the restaurant to join Sandhya at our table.

We're midway through eating when Sandhya sips her iced coffee and says, "I know that moving in together this summer is a really big deal. Is there anything you want to talk about as we're getting ready for the move?"

I nibble on the edge of a tortilla chip. "Like what?"

"Anything, I suppose. Like, do you always use a certain water glass? Or do you need complete silence to fall asleep? Maybe it sounds random, but sometimes those little things can be the most important on a day-to-day basis."

I eat another chip. "I don't want to be rude," I finally say, "but I don't like fancy soaps. The ones that smell like perfume."

"Like the ones in my apartment?"

"They're really nice," I say quickly. I don't want to offend her. But I'm also remembering how Maureen pointed out that people with Sensory Processing Disorder often have a hard time with strong smells. "I just think in my apartment—" I stop abruptly. "I mean, in *our* apartment . . ."

I trail off. I'm trying to think about how to describe the way scents make me feel. It's a horrible combination of itching down my spine and buzzing in my brain but I have no idea how to put that into words.

"I guess it's just the way I am," I finally offer.

"I totally understand," Sandhya says. "We can definitely switch to unscented soaps. Also, if you think of other things, please tell me. I'll ask Benji too. I know this is a big transition for you and your brother, and for Ruby too."

I go back to eating. The artichoke dip is really good. Most dips use mayonnaise, which tastes slimy in my throat, but this dip is made with tofu. Also, the artichokes are blended just right, not too chunky and not too soft.

"When you say *the way I am*," Sandhya says, scooping some dip onto a tortilla chip, "do you mean your sensory stuff?"

My cheeks flush. I never, ever talk about Sensory Processing Disorder with people who aren't my parents or Maureen.

"Yeah," I mumble. I crumple my napkin in one hand and reach for another.

"It's so interesting how your brain processes senses," Sandhya says. "I can't wait to learn more about you and help in any way I can." She glances at the napkins in my fists. "I know this is something you keep private and I will honor that. I haven't talked about it with Ruby, though I know she would understand and wouldn't judge you."

I'm not sure if she's asking for permission to tell Ruby. I quickly shake my head like *no, no, no, no, no*. It's one thing to have a confession torn in half on a piece of paper and another entirely to share this incredibly personal, often painful thing that makes me different from anyone else I've ever met.

Sandhya swirls her straw in her iced coffee. "Did you know that Ruby also struggles with things?"

"Like what?" I ask. Except when she's getting upset about graduation or having to pee all the time, she always seems so happy and easygoing.

"Do you know what anxiety is?" Sandhya asks.

I shrug. "Like being nervous?"

Sandhya nods. "I've raised Ruby as a single mom since she was a baby. It's always been the two of us, so a lot of nights she gets in my bed. She goes to sleep in her bed but wakes up and comes in. Ruby is excited about the marriage but she also tends to get anxious about certain things. As you can imagine, she's worried about what will happen when we all move in together and I'm married to your dad and Ruby can't climb in my bed anymore."

"Is that why she never wants to sleep over?" I ask.

Sandhya nods. "She hates sleeping away from me. I've talked it over with Ruby and she said it's okay if I tell you about her anxiety. She said it might even be a relief."

I nod, grateful that Ruby trusts me. "What about how she visits her dad in Michigan? She went over Christmas and she said she goes every summer."

Sandhya takes a deep breath and lets it out slowly. "It's hard. There are lots of tears and lots of calls. We've had to cut some visits short, or I fly out there and stay with them."

I arrange my napkins in a pile and stick my finger in the middle. I had no idea all that was going on with Ruby. Whenever I've slept over at her apartment we stretch out in sleeping bags, giggling for hours.

"I'm not saying you have to tell Ruby about your sensory stuff," Sandhya goes on. "I'm just saying that everyone has *things*. Your dad and I are going to work hard, along with your mom and Bill and Ruby's dad, to make sure that you and Benji and Ruby are all taken care of and that your individual needs are respected."

I smile at Sandhya. I like how she said that about her and Dad and Mom and Bill and even Ruby's dad. Five adults watching over us makes me feel safe and protected.

"Does Ruby know that I might live with my mom next year?" I ask. Dad told me that Sandhya knows it's something we're talking about. I haven't decided anything yet, and I don't have to for months. But it's definitely on my mind.

Sandhya shakes her head. "Not yet. No need to involve her in the conversation until we know more."

When we're done eating, we pile the plates and cups onto the tray. As she carries it to the recycling area, I go to the bathroom, where I use the dryer until my hands are warm and my brain is quiet. As I'm walking out to meet Sandhya, I think about that ocean poster from the guidance counselor's office. It said that in order to discover new lands you need to lose sight of shore. Maybe Ruby and I are a little lost at sea right now. But we don't need to be lost at sea alone. We can be on a boat together, paddling our way through the unknown.

CHAPTER 17

June finally arrives. I love June because it means the end of school and it also means I can get my KEENs! And KEENs mean no sock drama for at least three months. Whoever invented this amazing sandal-shoe is a genius because KEENs are 100 percent comfortable—the straps and the soles and even the toes. Mom always makes me wait to get my KEENs until June so they'll fit for the whole summer. On Sunday morning, we drive to a mall outside Tomsville. I pick out dark-purple KEENs so I can wear them with my graduation dress.

On top of the awesomeness of having new KEENs, Ms. Lacey surprises the class with a box of Munchkins during morning meeting on Monday. And then, on Tuesday, Avery isn't at school because she's shadowing a student at her new performing arts middle school. I know it's mean to be happy Avery is away but I can't help it. Another good thing about Tuesday is that Ruby is coming over after school, and so are Norie and Zoe Robbins. We've been asking for a while to all hang out after school together and finally this Tuesday everyone was free.

The four of us walk home with Joshua and Benji, talking and laughing the whole way. But then, as soon as we step into the apartment, I inhale sharply, trying to remember if I took down my checklists. School mornings are hectic and it's all I can do to remember my lunch and water bottle. As Joshua flicks on the lights, I quickly glance at the bulletin board. I'm relieved to see they're gone.

Ruby and the twins and I take turns jumping on the trampoline while Joshua makes us a snack of cookies and crackers and fruit. I can tell he's still feeling bad about moving to Chicago, even though I've told him I understand. He's apologized about ten times for springing the news on me, and he even gave me a special hairbrush for people with curly hair.

When we're done with our snack, we drift into my bedroom. At first we're all goofing around with my body sock. Norie and Zoe crawl in it together and roll across my floor and then Ruby and I give it a try, but she's short and I'm tall so we can't make it work. They don't ask what the body sock is or why I have it, which is kind of awesome.

After that, I give them a tour of my LEGO dog kingdom and they coo over my tiny plastic puppies. Then Norie and Zoe talk for about five minutes about this gorgeous sixth grader they saw when they went for a shadow day at their new middle school and how he looks like Tintin except with darker hair and how they're both desperately in love. I still haven't gotten a crush yet, not even a little bit. Ruby is nodding a lot and, for a few minutes, I get nervous that she's getting crushes now, too, and I'm the only one left behind, but when the twins leave to find the bathroom she whispers to me, "Please never let me be that boy crazy."

"I know!" I say, and we both heave a sigh of relief.

When the twins get back, Ruby and Norie and Zoe pull out their phones and start playing games and scrolling through memes.

I glance nervously at the iPad. I'm not supposed to get screen time in my room. I have it in here for calling my mom or listening to audiobooks, and we're allowed to have Minecraft on the couch on special nights. I wonder how the screen-time rules will change when Ruby lives here. Sandhya is a lot more laid-back about it.

"Screens away, everyone," Joshua says, opening my door. "And, yes, I know you had screens out because it suddenly got quiet in here."

Ruby and Norie slide their phones into their pockets, but Zoe is running her fingers across her screen.

"Can I show everyone one thing?" she asks. "It's really quick. I've been looking for it all over YouTube and I think I just found it."

Joshua shakes his head. "We don't do screen time in bedrooms. Willa knows the rules."

"It's a dog video," Zoe tells him.

"A dog video?" I ask excitedly.

Zoe nods. "It's so funny, Willa. You'll love it."

I can never say no to a funny dog video and Joshua knows that. We all lean in, Joshua included, and watch as this adorable Labrador retriever, Denver, gets in trouble for busting into a bag of cat treats. You can tell he's guilty because he's hanging his head low, but then, when his owner makes him look up, he grins bashfully with all his teeth like he's saying, *Sorry not sorry. Please love me anyway.*

We watch Denver a second time because he's so incredibly cute. Zoe is about to hit PLAY for a third time when Joshua shakes his head. "Awesome," he says. "But screens away."

"He's really nice," Zoe says once the door is closed.

"And cute," Norie says.

"You're lucky," Zoe says. "Our sitter is an old lady and she's mean."

Norie nods. "She yells at us."

"But he's moving," I say. "He's going to law school." I don't mention that I might be moving too. Mom and I have been talking about it when I go up there but we haven't made any decisions yet. It's definitely not something I'm ready to tell Norie and Zoe or even Ruby.

"When is Joshua moving?" Ruby asks.

"Summer. Like . . . August? He's going to Chicago."

Ruby frowns. "Wow. Another change."

"I know," I say.

Norie and Zoe are watching us curiously. Ruby nods at me and I nod at her and then I say, "We may as well tell you."

"It's big," Ruby says.

"What's big?" Norie asks.

I laugh nervously. "The thing is . . . Ruby's mom and my dad are getting married. No one else at school knows yet. We just found out a few weeks ago. The whole thing still feels really weird and—"

"That's so cool!" Zoe shrieks, cutting me off.

"You're so lucky!" Norie adds. "A true romance going on right before your eyes!"

"And you'll be sisters!" Zoe says.

Norie smiles. "Like us!"

"Everything okay in there?" Joshua calls from the living room.

"Everything's okay!" we all call back.

As Norie and Zoe ask us questions about how our parents fell in love and when they're getting married, I realize that it *is* okay. We *are* lucky. My dad could have gotten engaged to a woman with terrible children who fart a lot and have pet snakes. Or worse, a woman who has no children and always wants the house to be clean and quiet! Also, back in April, when Avery sneered at Ruby and me that we're becoming sisters, it sounded like an insult. But the way Norie and Zoe put it, it's making me excited. Maybe it is cool that I'm getting a sister.

"Can you be twenty percent okay with it?" Ruby asks like she's reading my mind.

"Eighteen percent," I say, grinning.

Zoe looks from Ruby to me like she's confused but then Norie knocks her twin's shoulder and, at the same time, they say, "Sister jokes!"

"Exactly," Ruby and I say, smiling at each other.

....

Thursday is Field Day. Our class starts out at the zoo, where Ruby and I search for the red pandas and giggle at the monkeys with the bare butts. I wish that, in addition to a dog, I could convince my dad to get me a monkey, but I know that's out of the question. We cross the path to the petting zoo, and Avery and I are the only kids brave enough to feed the sheep pellets from our hands. I actually like how their tongues feel on my palm. It's like rubbing my hand on the rough side of a sponge. When we're done, Ms. Lacey makes Avery and me slather in Purell and then wash our hands in the zoo bathroom.

By the time we get to the Great Hill, the whole class is in a good mood. We eat pizza and play Zombie Tag, and Ms. Lacey surprises us all with bracelets that say *I'm Outta Here* in black lettering. Some parents arrive with Popsicles and, as Avery helps pass them out to the whole grade, a group of us girls gather under a tree sucking our Popsicles and then digging in the grass with the wooden sticks.

A few girls are talking about their summer plans, like sleepaway camp or visiting grandparents in the Philippines, and some people ask Ruby and me about when we're moving in together. Ever since we told Norie and Zoe that our parents are getting married, it hasn't seemed like such a big deal to tell the others. It's not like we talk about it all the time, but I'm not trying to hide it anymore. I thought kids would think we're a freak-show family, but mostly they say it's really cool and that we're lucky.

"I found another Denver video," Norie says, pulling out her phone and holding it up for everyone to see.

We're not supposed to have screens at school, even on field trips, but when I glance over my shoulder I notice that the teachers are tapping on their phones too.

"Oh, I know Denver!" Avery says. She's back from delivering Popsicles, and she's leaning against a tree, showing off her fancy new phone. "I've watched all the Denver videos."

We all lean in and watch as Denver gets reprimanded for chewing Christmas ornaments. Then Zoe plays a video of a cat riding around his living room on a robot vacuum cleaner. Within minutes, everyone who has a phone is showing animal videos, and we're giggling and passing phones around, and it's all fun until I hear a girl from another fifth-grade class saying, "Oh my god, is that Willa?"

I glance over to see who's talking about me.

"Willa and I went to preschool together," Avery is saying as she holds up her phone. "This is from a holiday pageant."

I suck in my breath. The video has to be from when I was four and chucked my sneakers at the audience and tore down the string of Christmas lights. That's when my mom knew I needed help and she found Maureen for me. I've heard about the pageant and I've pictured it in my head, but I had no idea someone actually had a movie of it.

"Where did you . . . ?" I ask, but I'm so upset my voice catches in my throat.

"YouTube," Avery says. "When I got my phone my dad put his account on here, so I have all these videos from pre-school. I couldn't believe it. Willa, you were a crazy maniac."

"Can I see it?" Ruby asks, leaning in.

I stare at Ruby, horrified that she's betraying me by watching the video. But all of a sudden there's a commotion. Avery is shrieking and Ruby is running across the Great Hill. It takes me a moment to realize that Ruby has snatched Avery's phone out of her hands, and she's darting around people and trees and bikes like the awesome soccer star that she is. By the time Avery slides her feet into her sparkly shoes and pushes up from the grass, Ruby is out of sight.

A little while later, Ruby shows up again. She must have looped all around the Great Hill because she emerges on our other side. She's panting hard and her brown eyes are sparkling mischievously.

"Here you go," she says, tossing Avery's phone back to her.

"Be careful with my—" Avery pauses midsentence and

then, a moment later, she glares at Ruby. "It's gone! You deleted that video? You can't do that!"

It takes me a second to realize that Avery is talking about the preschool movie.

"You can't do that!" Avery says again. "It was on my dad's YouTube account. Now it's gone forever!"

Ruby crosses her arm over her chest. "I can and I did."

"I'm telling Ms. Lacey," Avery whines.

"Go ahead," Ruby says. Then she holds up her bracelet and points to the words *I'm Outta Here*.

I'm speechless. Seriously, my brain is not connecting to my mouth. If I could talk I would say to Ruby, *Thanks for doing that for me. It wasn't my fault that I was a crazy maniac back in preschool.*

And Ruby would nod. *Of course*, she'd say. *That's what friends are for.*

No, I would say to her, *that's what sisters are for.*

"Fine," Avery says. "Go ahead and be that way. I'll tell people your secret."

At the mention of the word *secret*, a few girls look up curiously from their phones. For a second I think Avery is going to tell everyone I have Sensory Processing Disorder. Leave it to Avery to figure that out somehow. Well, let her tell everyone. I'm sick of hiding it. I'll just say it's who I am and how I was born. Sorry not sorry.

Avery turns to Norie and Zoe. "Did you guys know that Ruby's mom and Willa's dad are together?"

Oh. That secret.

"That's old news," Ruby says.

"It's so romantic," Norie says.

"A true love story," Zoe adds.

Avery stands there, stunned.

"Come on," Ruby says, grabbing my hand and pulling me to my feet. "Let's play tag."

I'm tempted to stick my tongue out at Avery, but instead I skip across the grass to join a bunch of people playing on the hill.

CHAPTER 18

The next night, Dad, Benji, and I meet Sandhya
and Ruby at Ellington in the Park. That's an outdoor grill
in Riverside Park, on a patio above a large sandy area where
people play beach volleyball and swing from trapeze rings.
Dad often brings us there on warm Friday nights. This is the
first time we've been here with Sandhya and Ruby though.

They all order hamburgers and fries and I get a veggie
burger with melted cheese and potato chips. We're all talking
and joking around during dinner. I've noticed that Dad isn't
on his phone as much when Sandhya is around. Mostly we're
talking about summer vacation, but then Benji tells everyone
how he just read a book on celebrations around the world.
He wants to know what kind of wedding Dad and Sandhya
are having and whether they're going on a honeymoon.

"We're going to wait on a honeymoon," Sandhya tells him.
"We have enough to do with getting married and moving in
together. We'll all take some fun day trips later in the summer."

"We should go to Polar Bear Adventures for the honeymoon!" I offer.

Ruby nods enthusiastically. "You guys can get some 'me time' in the hot tub while Willa and Benji and I play in the water park."

"I still want to take you girls to Polar Bear Adventures for Ruby's eleventh birthday in August," Sandhya says.

I twist at the elastic on my KEENs. My arms and legs are starting to pulse with energy. If Sandhya and Ruby and I go to Polar Bear Adventures for Ruby's birthday, we'll all be living together at that point. We'll pack our backpacks and carry them out to the car, just like a family. Or maybe by then I'll be living with Mom and Bill during the week. I wish I knew what I was doing with that. Even though Mom and Dad keep saying we don't have to make the decision until the end of summer, I want to have it figured out.

"You should do a traditional Indian wedding," Benji says. "I've read that they take place over a few days and you can invite hundreds of people."

Sandhya shakes her head. "We're thinking more about City Hall in early July," she says, laughing. "Ten minutes and done. Just the five of us."

I nod approvingly. I like ten minutes and done. I've been to weddings, like even Mom and Bill's wedding, where you have to sit still for a solid hour. You can't even bring a book or people will think it's rude.

We've just finished eating our burgers when Benji slurps up the last of his water and suggests we play beach volleyball.

"The court is empty," he says, gesturing to the net on the far side of the sand pit. "There's even a ball down there."

"Why not?" Dad says, pushing back his chair. He takes Sandhya's hands and pulls her to her feet.

"It's been years," she says, holding on to Dad's hand, "but I used to be pretty good."

Ruby is already sprinting down the stairs and across the sand. I swear, if you say the word *ball* around Ruby it's like saying *bone* to a dog.

"Willa?" Dad asks, though by the way he's grimacing he knows that my answer is no. Dad is well aware that volleyballs and I are not friends.

"That's okay." I reach for my water.

"Come if you want," Dad says. "We won't be long."

I watch as Dad and Sandhya join Benji and Ruby at the volleyball net. It's kids versus parents. The sun is glaring over the Hudson River, so harsh it's making me squint. I'm sitting in a sharp metal chair watching this dream family: my dad and his soon-to-be wife and his sporty son and her sporty daughter. As if on cue, Ruby spikes the ball over the net, pumps her fist in the air, and high-fives my brother.

I suddenly want to donkey kick and flap my arms. But then, just as I'm about to lose it, a woman in exercise clothes walks by with a golden retriever lumbering after her.

She's just starting to tie the leash to a metal gate when I hurry over.

"Excuse me?" I ask. "I can watch your dog if you want. I love dogs."

"Sure," the woman says. "Katie would love that."

The woman hands me the leash and explains that she's going down to work out on the trapeze rings. She tells me that Katie is eleven and loves kids.

"Golden retrievers are my favorite dog," I tell her. I run my fingers over the bony bump on the top of Katie's head. I love golden retrievers' head bumps almost as much as I love the indent at the top of Cavalier King Charles spaniels' noses, just the right size to press your thumb in.

As I sit on the steps and pet Katie, I slowly start feeling better. Dogs are amazing that way.

"Hey," Ruby says, jogging over a few minutes later. "Cute dog."

"Her name is Katie," I tell her. "Her owner is over there on the rings."

Ruby plops down next to me and scratches behind Katie's ears. "She looks like that dog in the poster on your wall."

I nod in agreement. As Ruby wipes the sweat off her nose, I wonder if she came up here because she was tired of volleyball or because she wanted to be with me. Either way, I'm happy she's here.

"I once read that dogs' paws smell like popcorn," I tell Ruby. "Do you think that's true?"

"We can check," Ruby suggests.

I lift up Katie's paw and bury my nose in it, breathing deeply. "A little popcorny."

Ruby leans across me and goes next. "I just smell dirt."

"We could invent a new popcorn flavor!" I say, patting Katie's head. "We'd call it Dog's Paws."

"Yuck!" Ruby says.

"Thanks for yesterday," I blurt out. "For grabbing Avery's phone and deleting that movie. The video was from preschool. I looked like a total freak. I know you hate getting in trouble so I just wanted to say thanks for doing that for me."

"I didn't watch the video," Ruby says, shrugging. "I'm sure you didn't look like a freak."

"No . . . I did. It was from a performance where I threw my sneakers at the parents and ripped down the holiday lights."

Ruby snorts. "They probably deserved it for making little kids put on a show. I hate those performance things. I'm still nervous about fifth-grade graduation."

I nod, remembering our conversation in the school basement a few weeks ago.

"Even though we have our red-and-purple outfits," Ruby says, "I'm totally dreading it. I'm fine being watched on a soccer field. I don't get stressed about that. But being on a stage with everyone holding up their phones at us? I hate that."

I think about what Sandhya said when we were at that vegan restaurant, about how Ruby has anxiety about things. "I'll be up there on the stage with you," I tell her. "Does that help?"

Ruby scratches behind Katie's ears. "But you'll be in the back row with the tall kids. I'll be in the front with the short kids. Front and center for everyone to see."

"You could wear stilts," I offer. "Or platform shoes. Then Ms. Lacey will put you in the back."

"Or you could walk on your knees," Ruby says, laughing.

My dad, Sandhya, and Benji are still playing volleyball, and Katie is asleep at my feet, and the sun is sinking toward the river, and it's actually pretty, sort of golden and peaceful. All of a sudden I decide that it's time to tell Ruby. When Maureen suggested telling Ruby about Sensory Processing Disorder, I was like, *No way, I'll sound like a freak*. But maybe there are worse things than being a freak. Like keeping things bottled up. Like hiding who I really am.

"I was like that at the preschool performance because I have a disorder," I say to Ruby as I run my hand back and forth across Katie's back. "I've had it since I was little. It's even why I do some things now."

Ruby raises her eyebrows. "What kind of disorder?"

"It's called Sensory Processing Disorder. Mostly it means that being in my body is harder than it is for most people."

Ruby nods like she gets it, so I tell her that I see an occupational therapist after school twice a week and not a math tutor. I tell her how I hate some textures and smells and tastes and love others. I tell her about my checklists and charts and how hard it is for me to find comfortable clothes. I tell her that socks are evil, the worst invention ever.

"Is that why you had all those socks under your bed?" Ruby asks.

"Yeah," I say, nodding.

Ruby shakes her head. "I'm so sorry I made fun of you for that."

Just then, Katie's owner comes over and thanks us for watching her. Ruby and I hug Katie and kiss her about a thousand times before she slowly lumbers away.

"Why didn't you tell me all this before?" Ruby asks.

"I guess because it's embarrassing," I say. "It's private."

Ruby coughs. "I know my mom told you how I have a hard time with sleep, like how I'm scared to sleep alone. That's why I've never come for sleepovers. Sleepovers seem so easy for most people but I can't do them. I guess I'm a freak that way."

I sling my arm around Ruby's shoulder. "I don't think you're a freak."

"I don't think you're a freak either," she says, and then she rubs her eyes. It almost looks like she's crying.

"Are you okay?" I ask.

"I guess." She pushes her fists into her eye sockets. "Just a little tired. I don't know . . . I sort of don't feel well."

On the way out of the park, Ruby starts coughing really

hard. Sandhya buys her a bottle of water from a food cart. It helps for a bit but then she starts up again. She's still coughing when we get to Broadway and they descend down the stairs and into the subway.

....

I know something is wrong as soon as Dad walks in the door on Monday evening.

"Hey, Willa," he says, kissing the top of my head. His face is pale and his lips are pressed tight together. He turns to Joshua. "Where's Benji?"

"He's on a playdate with Max," Joshua says. "He's getting dropped off in a half hour."

"Oh, right," Dad says distractedly.

Joshua loads a few things in the dishwasher and slides his feet into his sneakers. The whole time Joshua is getting ready to leave, I watch Dad's face to see if I can figure out what's going on. I wonder if something went wrong at work? Or maybe he and Sandhya got in a fight and aren't getting married after all? When I think about that I feel a stab of sadness in my stomach and I suddenly realize that I actually like them together and I want it to stay that way.

As soon as Joshua is gone, Dad turns to me. "Willa."

He says it like a sentence with a period at the end, like he'd rather not keep going.

"What's wrong?" I ask.

"Let's sit on the couch," he says. "We need to talk."

Generally with things like this I get a burst of energy, but looking at Dad's face right now makes me go limp inside, like pasta that has been cooked too long. I sink onto the couch next to him.

"Sandhya took Ruby to the doctor today," he says.

"Yeah, Ruby wasn't at school. Did she get sick? She was coughing a lot in the park on Friday."

"She's not sick." Dad stares at his hands. I notice he's chewed his fingernails again. He gave that up two years ago. Benji and I celebrated by buying him nail clippers and several packs of gum.

"They went to an allergy doctor and did some tests," Dad continues. "They found out that Ruby is allergic to dogs. That's why she got sick in the park on Friday. You girls were petting that golden retriever. And remember Puppapalooza? How she didn't feel well and had to leave early?"

"But wouldn't they have figured that out before?" I ask, my voice rising.

"Ruby hasn't had a lot of exposure to dogs," Dad says. "Also, it sounds like she's gotten asthma attacks over the years and the allergy doctor says that's probably the reason."

"But she's already lactose intolerant! How can she also be allergic to dogs?"

"Those two things have nothing to do with each other," Dad says, rubbing my back.

"I know that," I say, clenching my teeth. "It's just . . . are they sure?"

My dad hangs his head. "Unfortunately . . . yes."

"So what about us?" I kick my heels back and forth against the couch. "What about our dog?"

"We're not positive," Dad says. "We've just learned about this."

"What about Manhattan Mutts? You already made the payment! The rescue dogs are arriving from South Carolina in a few weeks!"

"I need to call them and cancel," Dad says, "at least until we can think this through a little more."

"No!" I shout. I'm breathing fast and tears are flooding my eyes. "But you promised!"

"I know." Dad starts massaging his temples with his thumbs.

"What if I move up to Mom's?" I ask, but even as I'm saying it I realize a decision is forming in my head. "Then can I get a dog?"

"I thought about that, too, and I suppose it is a solution. I'll have to talk it over with Mom and Bill, only the dog couldn't come here along with you. As I said, we've only just found out, so—"

I don't wait for Dad to finish. I'm on my feet and running into my room, where I slam the door. This time when my golden retriever poster falls down, I rip it up and kick the pieces under my bed. Next I destroy my dog kingdom, knocking off dogs and pens and fences. I pause before tipping over the white poodle from Sophie, and then I push her over too.

"Willa," Dad says, knocking on my door. "Can I come in?"

"No!"

"Want to call Mom?" he asks. "Or even Maureen?"

"No!" I shout again. I hit PLAY on the iPad and crawl into my body sock, listening to *Old Yeller*. I'm right before the sad part where I always stop the story, but this time I keep listening, tears streaming down my cheeks.

CHAPTER 19

When I see Ruby at school the next day, she says hi and I say hi and it's out there, in the air between us, that *she* is the reason I can't get my dog. I know it's not her fault, so I'm not mad at her. But it feels sad and heavy like a towel that's been drenched with water and dumped in a heap on the bathroom floor.

It's the same on Wednesday and Thursday. Ruby and I eat lunch together and chat during classroom transitions, and we play follow-the-leader around the recess yard, and I get to be the leader. But we don't talk at all about the fact that she's allergic to dogs. It's like the elephant in the room. Or the 180-pound Saint Bernard.

On Friday morning, we walk quietly together up to the Maya A. orientation. Mr. Torres is the chaperone who brings us. All the Children's School students going to middle school there are invited in today for a tour and to see our sample schedules for the fall.

As soon as we walk into this enormous middle school, all long hallways and new faces, I start sliding my KEENs back and forth even though the soles are squealing loudly on the floor. I can't help it. I wish I'd brought gum. I wish I could do wall pushes right now or leap down a flight of stairs.

All of a sudden, I feel Ruby slip her hand in mine. "Sensory moment?" she asks in my ear.

"Totally," I say, squeezing her hand. When I was in kindergarten and my line partner used to complain that I was squeezing too tight, my teacher used to tell me to pretend there was a butterfly in the space between our hands. We always had to remember to maintain that pocket of space to keep the butterfly alive. I couldn't ever do it though. I always killed the imaginary butterfly.

Ruby squeezes my hand back. No space. All squished butterflies. "What helps when you're having a sensory moment?" she whispers.

The tour guide, the sixth-grade humanities teacher, is walking backward, pointing out the art rooms and the science labs. Kids in the classrooms peer out at us, and we look back in at them, like they're exhibits in the zoo called middle school. I wonder if any of them are kids we saw that day at I Scream when Dad and Sandhya told us the news. I can't believe how long ago that seems now. Also I can't believe Ruby and I are talking about the fact that I'm having a sensory moment. I've never talked about this with a friend before.

"This helps," I say tentatively, tugging at Ruby's hand. "And jumping. Also reading helps. It distracts my brain from my body."

Still holding my hand, Ruby raises her other arm in the air.

"Yes?" the humanities teacher asks, pointing at Ruby.

"You have a library here, right?" Ruby asks. "I saw it on the tour in the fall."

"We do," she says. "It's one of the things we're most proud of at Maya Angelou. It's got twenty thousand volumes of fiction, nonfiction, graphic novels—"

"Can we go there now?" Ruby asks. "Take a few minutes to look around?"

The teacher glances at her watch. "I suppose we can. It's one flight down and around the corner. Sure . . . why not?"

"Thanks," Ruby says to her. Then she whispers to me, "And let's jump the whole way down the stairs."

I smile at Ruby, my feet calm beneath me.

....

That afternoon, I call my mom.

"Everything okay?" she asks as soon as she answers.

We often don't talk on Fridays because we're about to spend the weekend together. But I decided something for sure today and I can't wait until tomorrow to tell her.

"I've decided I'm staying in New York City next year," I

say, "I want to stay here and go to Maya A. and keep coming to you on weekends."

"Okay," Mom says slowly.

"Are you mad?"

"Oh, Willa . . . of course I'm not mad. Dad and I only want what's best for you. It's been working just fine as is and we'll keep doing that."

"I'm going to call Dad at work," I say quickly before she can ask if I've told him yet. "See you tomorrow? I can explain more then."

"I can't wait," Mom says, and then we say good-bye.

As soon as Dad answers, I say to him, "I'm staying here in New York City and I'm keeping my room."

When Dad doesn't respond, I continue.

"I've thought about it and I love my room. It's my Girl Cave and I need it and it's really important to me. Also Benji and Ruby are both neat so they should share a room. And then Ruby doesn't have to sleep alone, which I know she doesn't like."

"I can see you've thought it all out," Dad finally says.

"I have," I say. I'm about to add *and I'm not changing my mind* but I know I can't do that. This is not just about me. It's Ruby's and Benji's lives, too, and they should get a say.

"It's funny," Dad says, "Sandhya was also saying that about the bedrooms. She and Ruby have been talking about it and Ruby doesn't want you to give up your room. Benji says he's okay either way as long as I install a chin-up bar in

212

the apartment. And you're right . . . Ruby and Benji do have similar, uh, sanitary styles."

"Meaning they're not slobs?" I ask, laughing.

Dad laughs with me. "That's one way to put it."

"I still feel really bad that Ruby is allergic to dogs," I say.

"I know you do," Dad says.

"It's not her fault . . . but I still hate it."

"I get it," Dad says. "I definitely do."

That evening, I'm stretched out on my bed reading Tintin when Ruby calls me on FaceTime. We don't talk a lot and, if we do, it's mostly making goofy faces back and forth into the screens.

She's sitting cross-legged on her bed, holding up the phone in front of her face, which is frowning and serious. "I'm going to tell the parents that you have to get your dog and I'll just take allergy medicine every day. Or I'll do those terrible shots."

"But you're really allergic," I say. "That wouldn't be fair to you."

"But it's not fair to you that you can't get a dog," Ruby says.

"I want a dog," I say, "but your friendship is more important."

"It's not an either-or," Ruby says.

"But if it has to be," I say, "I pick you."

Ruby smiles hard into the screen and I smile back at her.

It's sunny and hot on graduation day, almost ninety degrees. Ms. Lacey's class lines up on the left side of the auditorium for fifth-grade graduation. There's no air conditioning in here, so we're all fanning ourselves with whatever paper we can get our hands on. I'm wearing my red-and-purple dress and my purple KEENs, and my mom came over to the apartment before school to braid my hair.

We're in alphabetical order waiting to go up onstage, where the entire fifth grade is going to sing "That's What Friends Are For." Also the principal is going to make a speech and we're going to get our diplomas. I'm currently in the G-H-I part of the line, sandwiched on either side by boys. I can see Ruby up front with the A-B-C kids. She's wearing her red shirt and shimmery purple pants, and her hair is held back with a red-and-purple headband. As our parents took pictures of us outside school this morning, a lot of people told us that our color coordination looked awesome. I smiled and Ruby smiled and Mom and Bill and Dad and Sandhya held up their phones and took picture after picture after picture.

And I wasn't faking a smile either. I still love Ruby. And I meant what I said on the phone. If I had to pick between a dog and our friendship, I go with our friendship. That doesn't mean I don't feel sad about the rescue dog I'll never have, but losing my friendship with Ruby would be much, much worse.

"Welcome to the Children's School's fifth-grade graduation!" the principal says, leaning into the microphone and filling the auditorium with her voice. "I want to say a few brief words and then we'll get everyone up here and singing."

I crane my head to look at Ruby. She's frowning and hugging her hands to her stomach. I wish I could shout to her that it'll be okay, that she'll get through graduation just fine, but I don't want to get in trouble on my last day at The Children's School.

I glance into the audience. There, in the fifth row, I see Bill and Mom, then Benji, then Dad and Sandhya. Recently Benji has been calling us a blended family, and I kind of get it, all those parents and stepparents with the kids in the middle uniting everyone.

As I scan my eyes over the rest of the audience, I feel energy in my arms and legs but nothing wild. Nothing that's going to make me take off my KEENs and chuck them at the parents. Maybe Maureen is right. Maybe as I get older, Sensory Processing Disorder will feel easier, like I control it instead of it controlling me. When I saw Maureen on Monday, we did the dachshund-dog swing and some core strengthening on the yoga ball, and then she gave me a wrapped box with all my favorite things—Hubba Bubba gum and bracelets and even a pen where you can fidget while you're writing. She called it a good-bye-for-a-month present. She's on vacation now, and then Benji and I are going to Mom and Bill's for most of July. My mom has enrolled me in that LEGO camp that she was telling me about, and she's set up some sessions for me at the horse stable that does occupational therapy. We decided that even though I'm not moving there, it might be nice to try other kinds of OT.

I listen as the principal talks about The Children's School. I can't believe I'm leaving after spending more than half my life here. It's sad. Well, at least Benji will still be here so I can visit whenever I want.

"Fifth graders," the principal says, gesturing to the wings of the stage where we're all lined up, "come on up and let's commence graduation!"

I follow my line onto the stage. In graduation rehearsal, Ruby was put in the first row with the short kids just like she said, and I got placed in the third row with the tall kids. But as I pass Ruby, she looks so miserable that I'm concerned she might start crying. Even though Ms. Lacey is probably going to lecture me later about not going to my assigned row, I scurry over to Ruby and hold her hand and don't let go. So what that I'm the lone tall kid towering like a skyscraper over the front row? I'm there for Ruby and that's what's most important.

"Thanks," Ruby whispers, squeezing my hand.

I squeeze her hand back. Yet more squished butterflies.

"I really have to pee," Ruby says in my ear.

"Just ten more minutes," I say. "Can you hold it? Because if you can't I'll go to the bathroom with you. We'll get in trouble together."

"I think I can," Ruby says.

As soon as the ceremony is over, Ruby and I hustle to the bathroom. While she's in a stall, I wash my hands and then rub them on a paper towel. Back in kindergarten, these paper towels felt so scratchy I could barely touch them to my hands, but they're not so bad now.

In the classroom, the parents have set up a huge potluck breakfast. There's a long table covered with various foods— donuts, strawberries, bagels, cookies, even some random slimy cheesecake that I would never eat in a million years.

Dad and Sandhya are talking to the dad of a sporty boy. Ruby and a bunch of other kids are raiding the donuts. I'm standing with Mom and Bill, looking at the artwork on the walls, when a woman wearing glasses and an orange shirt appears in the door and starts talking to Ms. Lacey. I see them looking at me and pointing. I imagine it's someone coming to bust me for moving spots during the graduation ceremony, but then I notice Sophie standing behind the woman, clutching a homemade card in her hand.

"Are you Willa's mom?" the woman says, smiling and extending her hand to my mom. "I'm Jana. My daughter is Sophie. Willa has been wonderful with Sophie these past couple of months, building LEGOs together in Mr. Torres's office. We can't thank you enough for loaning us your daughter."

Mom looks questioningly at me. I hadn't even told her about my time with Sophie. It didn't seem like a big deal.

"Sophie talks about Willa a lot," Jana says. "Kindergarten has been a tough year for us. We're switching schools in the fall. We need a fresh start."

"Believe me," Mom says, "we've been there."

I glance down at Sophie. She's staring at her light-up sneakers, her hands clenched in fists. I totally remember when I was her age, listening to adults talk about my problems like I wasn't even there.

"Hey." I lean down so I'm level with her dark brown eyes. "It looks like you made me a card."

Sophie thrusts the card into my hands. Then she clutches her mom's elbow and tugs hard until her mom apologizes to us and leaves the classroom.

A few minutes later, Avery walks over to me. I assume she's going to say something nasty about my therapy sessions with Sophie. I brace myself by repeating *I don't care I don't care I don't care* in my head.

"Listen," Avery says quickly. "I'm sorry."

I'm so shocked it takes me a second to respond.

"For what?" I finally ask.

"For showing people that movie of you from preschool," Avery says. "I told my mom about it and she was mad at me. She said that some things should remain in the past."

I consider saying *It's okay*, but the truth is that it wasn't okay. Instead I just say, "Thanks."

Avery nods and stares down at her feet. I suddenly realize that she hasn't been as mean these past few weeks. In fact, there have been a few times when she's actually been nice, like once she handed me my pencil after I dropped it, and she was actually the one who nominated me for leader during follow-the-leader at recess.

I push my braids over my shoulders. "I want to thank you for something else," I say.

Avery looks up curiously at me.

"Thanks for not telling everyone about my dad and Ruby's mom."

"But at Field Day . . ." Avery stumbles. "I said—"

"You kept the secret when it was important . . . so thanks."

Avery touches her charm bracelet to her lips, and I realize she seems nervous, and not quite as intimidating as usual.

"I like your charm bracelet," I say. "Especially the dogs."

"Aren't you getting your rescue dog soon?"

Ever since my birthday in February I've been talking about my rescue dog to anyone who will listen.

"It's not happening right now," I say, shaking my head sadly.

Avery sucks in her breath. "What do you mean? You're not getting a dog?"

"I don't know," I say. "It's sort of up in the air."

"That's terrible!" Avery says.

The thing is, she looks genuinely sad. Avery is probably the only person I know who loves dogs as much as I do. My mom has always said that if we weren't enemies, Avery and I would probably be friends. I'm not so sure about that, but we definitely share the dog connection.

That's why I decide to be honest with her.

"You know how Ruby's mom and my dad are getting married?" I say. "Well . . . it turns out that Ruby is allergic to dogs so—"

"Willa," Avery says.

"And since they're moving into our apartment it means that—"

"Willa," Avery says, interrupting me again.

"It means that we can't—"

"WILLA!" Avery is practically shouting by this point.

"What?" I ask.

"My mom is an allergy doctor."

I'm about to roll my eyes like this is typical Avery bragging when I realize what she's saying. I ask, "Does your mom know about hypoallergenic dogs?"

"That's only her specialty," Avery says. "People come from all over the Tri-State area to work with her so they can get a pet even if they're allergic. She knows all about F1s and F2Bs and—"

Now it's my turn to cut her off. "I have no idea what you're saying, but can she talk to my dad and Ruby's mom, like, right now?"

"Of course!" Avery says.

Avery runs across the classroom and grabs her mom by both hands. She drags her mom over to Dad and Sandhya. "You guys need to talk allergies and dogs."

"Now!" I say, jumping up and down.

The grown-ups laugh like we're being cute, but Avery and I wait until they start talking, and then she reaches over to high-five me. I high-five her back. We're not going to be best friends anytime soon, but it's not a bad way to end our eight years together.

CHAPTER 20

A week later, Dad and Sandhya take the day off work and we drive down to City Hall. I've been to a few weddings before and I'm not a big fan. When I hear the word *wedding*, I think of itchy dresses and too-tight shoes, those long ceremonies that are impossible to sit still through, and dinners that are inedible except for the bread and butter.

That's why Dad and Sandhya's wedding is awesome. For a City Hall wedding, you go into an office, the justice of the peace says a few words, the people getting married say a few words, everyone signs paperwork, and it's done. It's faster than a parent-teacher conference! And you don't even have to dress up. Dad and Sandhya had this cool idea that we'd all pick on our own what we wanted to wear. The only rule was that we had to keep it secret from everyone else until that morning.

I decided to wear my graduation dress. It's comfortable and I like that Sandhya bought it with me. Benji showed up in his English Tudor Halloween costume from last fall, with a blue velvet jacket and a ruffled collar. Dad was in a flowered Hawaiian shirt and shorts. When we picked up Sandhya and Ruby at their building, Sandhya came out in a cream-colored sundress and Ruby was in her soccer uniform, without the shin guards.

It's kind of awesome, the looks we get as we leave City Hall and walk to a nearby Italian restaurant for lunch. We're all dressed differently and yet we fit together. Maybe that's what it means to be a blended family. Not blended like the guacamole from Noche Mexicana that's evenly mashed without the slightest lump, but blended in that we are all together but also uniquely ourselves. Dad must be thinking the same thing, because as soon as we sit down he raises his water glass and says, "A toast to our blended family!"

Ruby, Benji, and I grab our glasses and hit them into Dad's and Sandhya's. I find it impossible to clink glasses without spilling, and this time it's no different. The water sloshes out of my glass and pours down my arm.

"I have something I want to do," I say, rubbing my hand with a napkin. "You know how Mom and I do best part worst part every evening and that's *our* thing? I was thinking the five of us could have a tradition where we do rose, thorn, and rosebud every night instead."

"I did that at camp one summer!" Benji shouts.

"I know," I say, groaning. "I was at the same camp."

"What's rose, thorn, and rosebud?" Dad asks.

"Rose," I explain, "is your best part of the day. Thorn is

223

your worst part. And rosebud is something you're looking forward to. It can be tomorrow or even in the future."

"Can I go first?" Sandhya and Ruby say at the same time.

"Jinx!" Sandhya says to Ruby.

"Double-triple-pickle jinx!" Ruby says to her mom.

Dad and Benji and I laugh. It's funny to see how they have their own inside jokes. I hope they keep doing theirs and we keep doing ours and we also create new ones together.

"Rose," Ruby says, smiling at me, "is getting bonus siblings. Thorn is that I have to start packing for the move. Rosebud? Summer vacation!"

"I have the same rosebud!" Benji says.

"I have the same thorn," Sandhya says, groaning. "Not moving into your apartment. Just all the boxes and packing and sorting through stuff. We literally just did that last summer."

As the waiter comes to take our order, Dad and Ruby and Benji grumble in agreement that packing and sorting is definitely a thorn. I don't say anything because I'm not moving even one little bit. It has been decided for sure that I'm keeping my Girl Cave, and Benji and Ruby will be sharing the big room. They're actually really excited about it, and they've been talking all about how they're going to organize their things, and they're even planning a trip to The Container Store. I cracked up when I heard that and said that maybe while they're looking at containers I'd browse at the LEGO store a few blocks away.

We're just finishing our meal when Dad clears his throat. "I have one more rosebud," he says.

I glance quickly at Sandhya, who is grinning and nodding.

"Please tell me you're not having a baby," I blurt out.

"Definitely not," Dad says, laughing. "Remember I'm too much of a geezer to have a baby?"

"A geezer!" Ruby laughs so hard that she gags on her bread.

"So what's the rosebud?" Benji asks as Sandhya holds out a glass of water for Ruby to chug.

"Well . . ." Dad says.

Sandhya clears her throat. "The thing is . . ."

"Tell us!" Benji and Ruby and I all shout at the same time.

Before we can jinx and double jinx and triple-pickle jinx each other, Dad says, "We're going on a little road trip after lunch."

"Where?" I ask.

"We're going today?" Ruby asks.

Benji and I turn to her. "You know about this?"

Ruby shrugs. "Is it . . . ?"

Dad and Sandhya nod.

"Want to tell them?" Dad asks.

"Last weekend," Ruby says, "when you guys were at your mom's, we visited a family in New Jersey that Avery's mom knows. I did a trial session to make sure my allergies didn't flare up."

I rock backward in my chair. "A trial session with what?"

"Their goldendoodle!" Ruby grins at me. "And I was totally fine."

"That's half golden retriever and half poodle," Benji explains.

"I know what a goldendoodle is!" I tell him. Then I turn to Dad. "But why are . . ." I stumble, my brain moving too fast for my mouth. "I mean . . . why did Ruby . . . what's going on?"

"It turns out that Dr. Tanaka knows a family—some of her allergy patients. She helped them find a dog last year. It's a gorgeous, russet-colored, hypoallergenic goldendoodle. But the mom just got a new job in Hong Kong and they can't move the dog with them to Asia."

"Russet," says Benji. "That's reddish brown."

"I know what russet is!" I say. "Now can you please shut up already?"

"We don't say *shut up* in our family," Dad warns.

"What if Willa says *please* before *shut up*?" Ruby asks, giggling. "Does that cancel it out?"

"Ruby," Sandhya says in a warning tone. "That's enough."

I have to laugh. I think I might like having Ruby as my sister.

"They love their dog," Dad says. "She's easygoing and she's great with kids. But this is a permanent move to Hong Kong, so they've offered to give the dog to us. We can meet her today and then pick her up in two weeks, right before they leave."

I've heard of people being so surprised that they fall out of their chair, but it's never happened to me until now. One second I'm tipping backward and the next second I'm sprawled on the ground and my chair is sideways and waiters are scrambling over and everyone in the restaurant is staring at me. But I honestly couldn't care less if I look weird . . . because I'm getting a dog! A beautiful russet-colored goldendoodle! And thinking about that is much better than worrying about looking weird. One hundred thousand percent.

....

On the drive to New Jersey, Ruby and Benji fall asleep in the back seat—my brother at one window and Ruby in the middle—but there's no way I'm even a tiny bit tired. Dad and Sandhya have been filling me in on this family that has the dog. It turns out they also have two girls and a boy, just like us.

"So we'll bring the dog home in two weeks?" I ask.

"Yep," Dad says. "And Mom and Bill are on board to have it there as well. You'll come back to the city for a day or two in July, and I'll pick the dog up with you, and then we'll bring her right to Tomsville for the rest of the month."

"I really can't believe it," I say.

Dad smiles at me in his rearview mirror. "I know, Waggy. I'm so happy for you."

I don't correct him. This is definitely a Waggy moment.

Just then, Ruby opens her eyes, yawns loudly, and says, "Did you tell Willa about the problem?"

I tug at my seat belt, pulling it out far and letting it snap back onto my shoulder. "Problem?" I ask nervously. "Is it a big problem?"

Ruby shakes her head. "No . . . I guess it's a . . . crazy problem."

Sandhya glances back from the passenger seat. "Remember how the dog is reddish colored?"

"Russet," Benji says, rubbing his eyes.

"Well," Sandhya says, "another way to describe red is—"

"Do not tell me the dog is named Ruby!" I scream, bouncing in my seat. Seriously. This is so crazy there's no way I can sit still.

"Yep," Ruby says, grinning.

"It's true," Dad says.

I tug at my bracelets, twisting them and letting them go. "Can we change a dog's name?" I ask. "I mean, we can't have two Rubys in the family."

"And I'm not changing my name," Ruby says.

"You could," Benji offers. "Like, you could be Frida Kahlo. Or Rosa Parks. Or Joan of Arc!"

Ruby rolls her eyes like *yeah, no thanks.*

"I talked to a trainer," Dad explains, "and he said we can definitely teach a dog a new name, but he recommended we keep it to the same syllables and the same basic sounds. In this case, two syllables and end with an 'e' sound."

"But didn't you want to name it Oatmeal?" Benji asks.

"Oatmeal?" Ruby asks, wrinkling her nose.

"Willa and I have talked about breakfast-food names," Dad explains. "Maple, Cinnamon, Waffle—things like that."

"But none of those end with an 'e' sound," I say.

"I know a better type of food," Ruby says, grinning at me. "Our favorite!"

"Ice cream and sorbet with gummy bears on top?" I ask.

"Exactly," Ruby says. "What about Gummy Bear?"

"Gummy Bear," I say thoughtfully.

Sandhya turns again to look at me, and I can see Ruby and Benji watching me too.

"Gummy Bear would be her full name," Ruby says, "but we'd call her Gummy."

"No," Benji says. "Her full name would be Gummy Bear Kapoor-Garrett."

"What about your mom and Bill?" Ruby asks. "Gummy will be living there too."

"Anderson," I say. "That's my mom. And Bill's last name is Lucic."

"So, Gummy Bear Kapoor-Garrett-Anderson-Lucic," Benji says. "Definitely a blended-family dog."

"So it's official?" Dad asks.

I nod. "I love it."

Dad honks a bunch of times and we roll down the windows. "Gummy!" we call into the warm air. "We're on our way to meet you!"

"Get ready for your new name," Ruby shouts from the middle, "because Ruby is all mine."

"Get ready for your new family," Benji says out his window.

As we're screaming into the New Jersey countryside, I think about *Old Yeller*. I always paused the book before the sad part, but a few weeks ago when I listened until the very end I actually loved the last chapter. Travis sees the speckled puppy, Old Yeller's son, running wild around the house. You know, then and there, that Travis is going to fall in love with this new puppy. What I'm thinking about now is that if I hadn't listened to the sad part that made me cry, then I never would have gotten to the happy ending.

Maybe that's what life is like, that you have to survive the sad to get to the happy.

"Gummy!" I scream out the window so loudly that my voice cracks. "Here we come!"

There's a brief silence, and then a dog somewhere outside barks a bunch of times, almost like it's responding to me.

Acknowledgments

Thanks to:

My son Miles Rideout for giving me permission to tell your story of Sensory Processing Disorder through Willa, for making me a better parent, and for helping me realize that all the ways I've felt Invisible Weird my whole life aren't that weird after all.

My son Leif Rideout for being your unique and awesome self. You *own* it and I love you for that.

My husband, Jonas Rideout, for always encouraging me to write the book that is in my heart.

My editor, David Levithan, for nurturing Willa and Ruby, and to the superb team at Scholastic including Maya Marlette, Nina Goffi, and Christopher Stengel.

My agent, Jodi Reamer, for making it all possible, and to everyone else at Writers House including Alec Shane and Cecilia de la Campa.

Lori Rothman, for giving me a tour of your sensory gym and for talking with me about occupational therapy and Sensory Processing Disorder.

Phoebe Fried and Flora Jansche for answering my questions about life in fifth grade.

My early readers—Dianne Choie, Jackie Barney, Julia Barney, and Dr. Vijayeta Sinh—for giving me your valuable feedback.

My family and friends—you love me for who I am and I am forever grateful.

I tried to capture a child with Sensory Processing Disorder based on my son's experiences and my own; however, SPD manifests itself differently in every person. If you or someone you love is struggling with sensory issues, please know that you are not alone. There are many resources out there to help you—start with your pediatrician or a counselor at your school. Also remember that what often feels like your worst weaknesses will turn into your greatest strengths.

About the Author

Carolyn Mackler is the Printz Honor–winning author of the middle-grade novel *Best Friend Next Door* as well as several novels for teenagers. Carolyn's books have appeared on bestseller lists and been translated into more than twenty-five languages. She lives in New York City with her husband and two sons.